"I just wish he'd go te____

"Someone should do some____ ____ on the way to our next class.

"Drop a live wire in his fish tank," suggested Vinnie, baring his teeth in a repulsive grin. "Zap!"

As usual, Jill pretended he didn't exist.

"He's the worst teacher in all of Morgan Middle School," muttered Jill.

"Maybe Mr. Fisher doesn't eat breakfast." Rachel looked from Jill to me. "One of my magazines says that can make your blood sugar so low you can barely operate."

"We could bring him granola bars," I offered. "Poisoned ones."

"I vote for a fish fry." Vinnie smacked his lips.

"Naw," said Greg. "Wreck his stupid flowers."

"Steal his supply of pop quizzes," suggested Chris.

"Forget the quizzes," I said. "Take his grade book."

When Jill studied me thoughtfully, I added, "We could change all our grades to A's."

"And give my mom a heart attack?" said Vinnie. "No way."

OTHER PUFFIN BOOKS YOU MAY ENJOY

WHAT HAPPENED IN MR. FISHER'S ROOM

NANCY J. HOPPER

PUFFIN BOOKS

PUFFIN BOOKS
Published by the Penguin Group
Penguin Putnam Inc., 375 Hudson Street, New York, New York 10014, U.S.A.
Penguin Books Ltd, 27 Wrights Lane, London W8 5TZ, England
Penguin Books Australia Ltd, Ringwood, Victoria, Australia
Penguin Books Canada Ltd, 10 Alcorn Avenue, Toronto, Ontario, Canada M4V 3B2
Penguin Books (N.Z.) Ltd, 182-190 Wairau Road, Auckland 10, New Zealand

Penguin Books Ltd, Registered Offices: Harmondsworth, Middlesex, England

First published in the United States of America by Dial Books for Young Readers,
a division of Penguin Books USA Inc., 1995
Published in Puffin Books, 1997

1 3 5 7 9 10 8 6 4 2

THE LIBRARY OF CONGRESS HAS CATALOGED THE DIAL EDITION AS FOLLOWS:
Hopper, Nancy J.
What happened in Mr. Fisher's room / by Nancy J. Hopper—1st ed.
p.   cm.
Summary: Lanie has lots to deal with in eighth grade—a new friend, boys,
and most of all Mr. Fisher's out-of-control science class.
ISBN 0-8037-1841-1
[1. Teacher-student relationships—Fiction. 2. Schools—Fiction.
3. Behavior—Fiction.] I. Title.
PZ7.H76915Wh 1995 [Fic]—dc20 94-41656 CIP AC

Puffin Books ISBN 0-14-038076-0

Printed in the United States of America

WHAT HAPPENED
IN MR. FISHER'S ROOM

1

The week we kids finally decided to do something about Mr. Fisher, Monday's sixth-period science class began as usual, with kids making animal sounds and Vinnie Charles acting like a clown. The major difference was that the test Mr. Fisher gave was announced instead of a pop quiz. Another difference was that I was better prepared than normal, having spent hours studying the effects of the Ice Age on our earth.

When I finished the test, I settled back in my chair, watching the watery March light filter through dirty windows. Then, as I started to daydream, taking real people and real events and rearranging both to make them more interesting, someone knocked a book off a desk. Someone else, near the hall door, made birdlike twitters. Chad Jeffers, a skinny kid who barely comes to my shoulder, snorted softly through his nose.

I eyed Mr. Fisher. He was leaning against his

desk, his arms folded over his chest, looking almost as relaxed as he had last fall. He'd been a new teacher then, in a lot of ways like a big dumb dog who doesn't know when to be friendly and when not to. Not dumb, I corrected myself, remembering how Mr. Fisher could lecture on and on about science without looking at the book. He had to be smart to have learned all those facts. Unfortunately, he expected us to learn them too.

As he glanced in my direction, I picked up my pencil, then moved the test on my desktop, reread several of my answers, and yawned. One more period and school would be over for the day.

Vinnie, who sat next to me, was hunched over his paper, writing his answers in red pen. When he finished, he began to draw a stick figure at the top of the page, next to the big red F he'd scrawled to save Mr. Fisher the effort.

The figure reminded me of Vinnie, all long meatless bones and awkward angles. Then Vinnie added a large head and I knew it couldn't be. Vinnie has a pinhead with eyes like small cloudy brown marbles, but the head in the drawing was square with large eyes, a narrow mustache, and a dimple in the chin. When Vinnie drew a curl drooping on the forehead and added a raised hand to brush the curl back, I was certain he'd drawn our teacher. What was better was that next Vinnie drew a female figure beside him.

If I leaned to the left, I could see tight curls on the head, curls like Anne Mastrianni's, but I couldn't quite read the name Vinnie was printing under the figure. I leaned farther, holding onto my desk so I wouldn't fall out of my seat.

"Melanie!"

Through a violent convulsion of my upper body, I remained in my seat. I drew a deep breath and pushed my glasses up on my nose.

Mr. Fisher's eyes were unreadable, but the muscle along the line of his jaw twitched. "Give me your paper," he said.

"I wasn't looking at his answers," I protested.

"I saw you."

"Me? Cheat off Vinnie Charles? You have to be kidding!" I couldn't *believe* Mr. Fisher. I mean, *nobody* would copy from Vinnie.

"Copycat," said Vinnie. "Meow. Purrrrr."

In the back of the room somebody brayed like a donkey. Three rows to my right, Chad snorted more loudly.

Mr. Fisher turned red, but he held out his hand. "Give me your paper," he repeated, "and move to the seat behind Anne."

5

"Gee, thanks," I blurted. "Now when I want to cheat, I'll be sitting next to Jill. I'll get all A's."

Mr. Fisher continued to hold out his hand.

I gave him my test, then gathered my books, stomped three steps forward, and slammed them on the desk behind Anne. "It's just not fair," I snarled under my breath, sliding into the seat. I glared at Mr. Fisher, then deliberately turned sideways to watch Jill, who was checking her answers.

Jill is small and delicate. Only her brown eyes are large, accented by the chestnut hair she wears parted in the middle to fall like a curtain around her face. Her skin is so pale it looks as if the slightest touch will bruise it, but despite her fragile appearance Jill is fun to be with. She's smart too. She has a perfect A average.

As for me—I look revoltingly healthy, the type who would have married early in pioneer days because my true love figured that in a pinch I could help pull the wagon over the mountains. Not that I'm fat. I prefer to think of myself as big-boned. I'm also rather tall for my age, with long semiblond hair. My eyes are blue behind large pink-framed glasses, which I plan to exchange for contact lenses in the near future.

While Mr. Fisher collected test papers, he gave

our assignment. Because the animal noises had picked up volume, he had to speak loudly to be heard.

"You should know the terms having to do with rock formations and shale," he told us.

"Erk-a-doodle-doo!" came from the direction of the pencil sharpener.

I waited while Jill wrote the assignment in the small notebook she carries for that purpose. Since September, when my best friend, Mary Beth, moved to Kalamazoo, Michigan, Jill had been my closest friend—although Rachel Porter and I got together during school. After school, Rachel always seemed to be with a boy or baby-sitting her little brother.

"I really studied for that test," I grumbled as Jill and I left the room. "I know I had at least a B."

"Go see Mr. Fisher after school," she suggested. "If you're real nice and apologize, he might not fail you on the test."

"I don't know. . . ."

"Go on." Jill smiled encouragingly. "Even Mr. Fisher has to know nobody in their right mind would copy answers from Vinnie."

I shifted my books in my arms. "I can't stand that man," I said.

"Who has to like him? I'm talking about saving your grade."

"I always get the feeling in there that it's us against him," I muttered, shoving my glasses up with my free hand.

When Jill made a wordless sound, I decided it was times like this I missed Mary Beth the most. Jill didn't understand me, not the way Mary Beth did. Jill seemed to think a big part of life boiled down to whether you got perfect grades or not. Sometimes I thought she didn't much care about other things, such as how you felt about yourself. I mean, how could I possibly go begging to Mr. Fisher when I didn't even like him?

"I hate Mr. Fisher," I said to myself as Jill went to gym and I entered wood shop on the opposite side of the hall. "I really do."

2

———⊰🐟⊱———

I didn't go to see Mr. Fisher after school and Jill didn't say anything more about it. Instead, as we slid into our regular seats on the bus, she started talking about her older sister, Amy.

"And Dad took away her car keys for the whole week," she finished with satisfaction. "She's not even allowed to drive to cheerleading practice."

Although Jill sounded pleased Amy was in trouble, I wasn't much interested. I was still brooding over the fact that Mr. Fisher had taken my paper and that now I'd get an F on the test. I'd been counting on that test to pull up my science grade.

"See you tomorrow," said Jill, standing to get off the bus, "if I don't call you tonight."

"Good luck at the dentist," I told her.

"Thanks."

My stop was five blocks from Jill's. That gave me a chance to become even more depressed. I didn't much care to hear about Amy, but Jill's chatter was better than being stuck with my own thoughts. To make things worse, the sky'd become overcast since morning, and a cold drizzle began to fall as I swung down off the bus. I slung my book bag over my shoulder and trudged the half block home, then ran up our front steps as the rain became a downpour.

The cement floor of the porch was as wet as if it had rained all day. I checked the mailbox for a letter from Mary Beth, but all it contained was a grocery-store ad and a bill from the electric company. Then I opened the storm door and reached for the knob on our big front door.

The knob didn't turn. That meant that not only was Mom not home but Sophie, my older sister, wasn't either. "Figures," I said out loud. "Any time I need to dump on someone, nobody's home." I searched my purse, found my key, and in another minute was inside.

The living room was as dark as night. Without pausing to turn on a light, I went straight to the kitchen. I dropped my book bag and my coat on the nearest chair and crossed to the refrigerator. On its front was a note held down by a magnet in the shape of a piece of chocolate candy.

"Showing a house at four," it said. "Please put the casserole that's in the fridge in the oven at 350° at four-thirty." The note was signed by my mother. Under "Mom" she had written three X's and two O's.

I don't need X's and O's, I thought bitterly. What I need are real hugs and kisses. I opened the refrigerator door and stared inside, then took out a can of orange pop and went to sit at the kitchen table. Slowly drinking it, I brooded over Mr. Fisher and my test and then about how my life had deteriorated since Mary Beth moved away.

Not as much as Mary Beth's life had, I tried to remind myself, but I wasn't so sure. At first Mary Beth had sent me lots of letters, saying how much she missed me and the good times we'd had together. But by Thanksgiving the spaces between letters were greater, and she'd begun to write about the new friends she was making. Since Christmas I'd been lucky to get one letter a week, and the pages seemed filled with the names of kids I didn't know.

Mary Beth doesn't miss me anymore, I thought, and tears formed in my eyes. She doesn't know there's this big hole inside me where our friendship used to be. She thinks my life's just going on the way it used to, but nothing's the same any more—not school, not my friends, not even my family.

That wasn't entirely true. My dad was the same big old growly bear he had always been. But I hardly ever saw my mother since she'd started a job selling real estate. She got off work about the same time as Dad, and the two of them talked all through dinner to each other. A lot of evenings Mom went back out to show a house, and she was gone most every Saturday, sometimes on Sunday too.

Of course I did have Sophie to talk to, when she was around. But at the moment she was in a play, so she was at rehearsals every night after school. When she arrived home, everybody else would be here too, and I didn't exactly want to announce my latest science failure over dinner.

"You have Jill," said a voice inside my head. The voice was like Mary Beth's when I'd called her in October and mentioned I was hanging around with Jill. Mary Beth had sounded sulky, and I'd realized with a start that she was jealous.

"Jill," she'd repeated, as if she didn't believe me. Then she'd added, "I never thought you were Jill's type."

"Don't worry," I'd said. "We'll never be as good

friends as you and me. I just get so lonely sometimes."

Five months later I was still lonely. I finished drinking my pop, rinsed out the can, and threw it into the recycling bin.

Then I had a super idea. I could phone Mary Beth that very minute. My eyes flicked to the kitchen clock and then to the telephone on the wall by the kitchen table. Mom wouldn't care, not if I offered to pay for the call out of my allowance.

Probably Mary Beth isn't home, I thought as I dialed her number. Probably she's at a mall with some of her new friends. Probably—

"Hello," said a familiar voice.

"Mary Beth!" I shrieked.

"Lanie!"

"How are you?" I asked her.

"Great. I mean, fine. I mean, I miss you, but everything's okay here. What about you?"

"Terrible," I moaned, although already I was feeling better. "Awful. I *failed* a science test today."

"Oh, Lanie."

"It wasn't my fault," I blurted. "Mr. Fisher took my paper. He said I was cheating."

"Come on . . ."

"He thought I was copying off Vinnie Charles."

"Vinnie? Are you kidding?"

"I wish," I said. "Of course Mr. Fisher made a fool of himself, because everybody knows I'd never copy from Vinnie. But that won't help my grade."

There was a little silence. Then Mary Beth said, "Gee. That's awful."

"Everybody has problems with Mr. Fisher," I told her. "He has no control at all. The room is like a zoo. It even sounds like one. Kids make animal sounds all through class."

When Mary Beth didn't answer, I added, "You're lucky you missed him."

"Hey!" Mary Beth sounded as if that reminded her of something. "Guess what?"

"What?"

"Mother's going to let me visit you the whole last week of June."

"Oh, Mary Beth!" In an instant I forgot about my test, Mr. Fisher, and science class. "That's terrific! Maybe Mom'll let me have a party with all the kids. It'll be just like old times."

"For sure!" agreed Mary Beth; and for a little while, it was like old times, the two of us on the phone, making plans. By the time I hung up, it was as if my failing a science test was something that had taken place a long time ago. All I could think about was Mary Beth's visit.

Later, I often wondered what would have happened if Mary Beth hadn't been home, if instead I'd talked to my parents about my problems in science class. Would Mom and Dad have met with Mr. Fisher or gone to the principal? Would I—somehow— never have been involved in what happened in Mr. Fisher's room?

3

ince there were no as-
signed seats in the cafeteria, I always sat with Jill,
Rachel, and some of the other kids at lunch. While
we ate, we joked, gossiped, and made plans for later.
It was my favorite period of the day.

But on Tuesday, lunch got even better—or so I
thought. Chris Randall came to our table, sitting beside Rachel and across from me. I didn't really care
that the big attraction was Rachel. While Chris eyed
Rachel from under his long dark lashes, I could watch
him.

Because Jill was my best friend now, I'd told her
I thought Chris was the cutest boy in the whole
eighth grade. Every so often during lunch, Jill would
nudge my foot with hers. Then I'd nudge her back
and we'd both giggle.

"What's so funny?" Chris asked when Jill and I'd
been giggling more than usual.

"Nothing." I tried not to grin.

"Nothing at all," Jill said airily.

"Where are you going to ride your new ATV?" Rachel asked him.

"At my uncle's," Chris said. "He has a bike trail on his farm, at the edges of fields and through a pine woods."

"Sounds like fun," Rachel said. The way she was watching Chris reminded me of a picture I'd seen of a cobra. The snake had raised the top part of its body. Its eyes were intent on its prey, its mouth slightly open to show sharp fangs with a little pink tongue flicking out between them.

"You want to come along sometime?" asked Chris.

Rachel picked that moment to lick her lips.

I dissolved into helpless giggles.

Chris looked at me, confusion drawing his dark brows together so they almost met. Then he reached for his milk carton. Because he was staring at me, he missed. His hand knocked into the carton and sent it tumbling.

A stream of milk poured across the table. It soaked my pumpernickel, cheese, and pickle sandwich, then rushed on to splash down the front of my red top.

"Sorry!" Chris jumped to his feet and threw his

napkin in the puddle of milk. Then he leaned across the table, grabbed Rachel's napkin, and began dabbing at the spot on my top.

I had a close-up view of his blond spiky hair until Chris realized he was almost touching my breast. He turned red and sank back into his seat, where he remained with his eyes fixed on his tray until the bell rang.

At least Chris noticed me, I told myself. In science class the following period I rested my chin on the palm of one hand and began to daydream about the two of us.

Since the school's heating system hadn't adjusted to the change in the weather, the room was hot and stuffy. The noise was worse than usual too, maybe because Mr. Fisher hadn't finished correcting our tests, giving us a vacation from bad grades.

The rooster near the pencil sharpener kept interrupting my daydreams. He didn't do much for Mr. Fisher either. Mr. Fisher tried to catch whoever was crowing but couldn't. Whenever he moved in that direction, bird twitters would begin on the opposite side of the room, forcing him back the other way.

"Melanie?" said Mr. Fisher. He's the only person who calls me that. Everyone else calls me Lanie.

"Hunh?" I was unaware he'd asked me a question.

"What did our textbook call 'layers of earth'?"

"Layers?" Why was he picking on me?

"Strata," he said. "You ought to know that."

When the other kids laughed, my cheeks flooded with heat and I wanted to shrivel up from embarrassment. Of course I knew the answer; *Strata* is my last name. Scowling at Mr. Fisher, I slumped low in my seat. It was his fault I'd forgotten the answer. Nobody could concentrate with all the noise in the room.

Chad snorted softly through his nostrils. As Mr. Fisher glanced at him, the rooster crowed again.

"All right, Chad. You get two detentions."

I rolled my eyes at the ceiling and sighed loudly. At once the room filled with sighs. I glanced at Jill, who raised her brows, then looked quickly back at the teacher.

Why can't Mr. Fisher control our class? I wondered with disgust. Mrs. Aston, who couldn't top one hundred pounds wearing ankle weights, never let anybody get away with anything in Language Arts. I listened for several minutes, absorbing information about the earth, then gazed at the three African violets on the windowsill, trying to fantasize their brilliant reddish-purple flowers into the background of another daydream. It was no use. A note of despair in Mr. Fisher's voice brought me back to reality.

"What *is* the strata of the earth composed of?" he asked.

He doesn't expect us to know, I realized. Mr. Fisher is over six feet tall and had to weigh more than my father, but at that moment he seemed small to me. He pushed his curl back from his forehead and said, "Hasn't anyone been listening?"

"No!" said Vinnie and laughed since that is his idea of a really witty comeback.

"Jill?"

"Unh, rock."

"Good."

"And sand."

There was a short silence. Then the bird song began again near the door.

"Will the thrush hush!"

Evidently Mr. Fisher didn't understand he was funnier than Vinnie. He looked bewildered when the class erupted into laughter.

Vinnie laughed longer than the rest of us, even after Mr. Fisher told him to shut up.

"It's funny," said Vinnie, a big grin splitting his thin face.

"Settle down."

"But you made a joke."

"I—"

"Why are you arguing with him?" For a second I didn't realize who'd spoken. Then, with a sinking feeling, I knew. My big mouth, curse of my life, had taken over again. "Why don't you give him a detention?" I added, trying to sound helpful instead of sassy.

"Yeah," said Vinnie. "Give me detention."

Chad snorted and the rooster crowed. Someone began to stamp his feet on the floor. Within seconds the floor trembled from the pounding of many feet.

When all else fails, Mr. Fisher gives us one of the pop quizzes he keeps ready in his desk drawers. It was apparent we were due for another one when he turned toward his desk.

"Oh, no," breathed Jill.

"Anyone talking during the quiz will receive a zero on it and for today's class participation," Mr. Fisher announced as he distributed papers.

I avoided his blue eyes, which looked as bleak as his voice had sounded. Instead I took the stack of tests Anne passed over a shoulder, dropped one on my desk, and passed the rest on to Anthony Everette, who sits behind me.

The questions covered the material Mr. Fisher had been discussing in class. I read them doubtfully, having been immersed in my daydreams while he talked. Beside me Jill made a little sound, a cross between a whine and a groan. She's deathly afraid she might get a B in science this marking period, the first blemish ever on her perfect record.

Personally, I think a few B's and a sprinkle of C's is a sign of an independent mind. But D's and F's— I bit my lower lip and filled in the blanks I could.

It didn't take long. When I put down my pencil, I leaned my chin in the palm of my hand again to stare at the fish tank in front of the bulletin board. In it three black lace angels, a silvery discus, and a little gray catfish swam serenely among water plants. The aerator gurgled cheerfully.

Usually when I watch the fish, my muscles loosen and I feel a gradual easing in my mind too, like a fist slowly opening. But that afternoon I couldn't relax. I was too angry at Mr. Fisher for making me open my big mouth and too upset by the atmosphere in the science room. The animal sounds and the quizzes weren't funny. That class was ugly, with the students baiting the teacher, and Mr. Fisher responding with more detentions, more quizzes, more frustration, and more despair.

I glanced at Jill, who had her pencil grasped tight enough to whiten the knuckles of her fingers. Her pale face was drawn in an expression of dismay, and Jill was the best student in the whole school.

Science class was ugly all right, and it was Mr. Fisher's fault, because he couldn't control us. As for us students—our behavior was growing more daring and more hateful as the days passed. It was almost as if we were trapped on some sort of treacherous sliding board, and we'd been hurtling recklessly down the board for weeks.

What I didn't realize that gray afternoon in late March was that we hadn't reached bottom yet.

4

Someone should *do* something about that man," Jill said on the way to our next class.

"Drop a live wire in his fish tank," suggested Vinnie, baring his teeth in a repulsive grin. "Zap!"

As usual, Jill pretended he didn't exist. Anne, who was tagging along with us, turned her mouth downward in disgust.

When we reached the gym, Chris and Greg were standing in front of the door. Chris didn't look at me, but at least he didn't leave. Greg made a low crowing sound.

"Oh, you're the rooster in science class!" I stopped and stared at him.

Greg grinned in response. His hair was brownish red like a chicken's feathers, but there all resemblance ended. He was almost my height, with a sturdy build, and had green eyes and a splatter of orange freckles across the bridge of his nose.

"That whole class is depressing," said Anne.

"I just wish he'd go teach somewhere else," I told her.

"Who?" asked Chris.

"Mr. Fisher," explained Jill.

"Oh, him."

"He's ruining . . ." began Jill, then stopped.

She'd been about to say her perfect grades, I realized, but she hadn't, maybe because Vinnie always had horrible grades and Anne was no record setter either. Noticing the angry tinge of pink in Jill's pale cheeks, I said, "I could only answer three questions."

"It's the noise," said Anne. "It gives me a headache."

"Oh, go away." Jill waved a hand in Anne's direction. "You give *me* a headache, hanging around all the time."

When Anne's eyes flew wide, I glanced away. Anne should have realized Jill was in a bad mood. We all were.

"He's the worst teacher in all of Morgan Middle School," muttered Jill.

Rachel, who had just arrived from math, asked, "Who are you talking about?"

"Three guesses." I moved to make room for her.

Rachel shook her head, then said, "Mumbles Mitchell?"

"Mr. Fisher," I told her.

"He's not so bad."

"He's awful," said Jill.

"Chelsea Zeller likes him."

"Chelsea'd like anybody who knows about plants and animals," I pointed out.

"Maybe Mr. Fisher doesn't eat breakfast." Rachel looked from Jill to me. "One of my magazines says that can make your blood sugar so low you can barely operate."

"We could bring him granola bars," I offered. "Poisoned ones."

"I vote for a fish fry." Vinnie smacked his lips.

"Naw," said Greg. "Wreck his stupid flowers." He crowed like a rooster again. He was getting better at it.

"Steal his supply of pop quizzes," suggested Chris.

"Forget the quizzes," I said. "Take his grade book."

When Jill studied me thoughtfully, I added, "We could change all our grades to A's."

"And give my mom a heart attack?" said Vinnie. "No way."

Somehow it was difficult to think of Vinnie with a mother, especially one who'd stuck by him for thirteen years. While I was trying to imagine her, Chris said, "It'd be easy to steal his grade book. He always keeps it in the top left drawer of his desk."

"Since everybody hates him, they'd never narrow the list of suspects to one person," said Jill.

"I don't hate him," Rachel protested, but no one paid any attention to her.

"Let's all bring salt to school tomorrow," said Chad, who'd been listening in for the past couple of minutes. "One person can salt his stupid violets, but not tell anyone else. We'd all be guilty, but innocent too."

"Tomorrow's too soon," I pointed out, thinking that at least one person would be guilty. "If we wait until Monday, we can get more kids in on it."

"Great plan," said Chad. "Super."

"Right," agreed Vinnie.

Greg practiced another crow, louder.

It was then that Mr. Gembar stuck his head out of wood shop and asked, "Lanie, Rachel, are you coming to class?" Mr. Gembar didn't mention Vinnie, maybe in the hope that Vinnie would skip shop.

"Mr. Gembar likes girls," said Vinnie, following us into the room. "Eighth-grade girls."

If Mr. Gembar heard Vinnie, he ignored him. He went to the front of the room to repeat the lecture he gives on safety practically every day.

"Students using saws, put on your safety glasses and go stand by the saw tables," he said after his lecture. "I'll come around to unlock them. The rest of you, remember to apply your varnish slowly with a light touch."

I picked up the decorative paddle I was making for Mother's Day. Since I'd brushed the varnish on too quickly, my project was a mass of runs and bubbles, which no amount of sanding seemed to remove. I picked up a piece of sandpaper.

While I sanded, I watched Mr. Gembar unlock saws and listened to Rachel. She was gouging a series of lines in the wood of a jewelry box she'd made as she chattered about her big decision whether to go to Saturday night's skating party with Chris or some boy in the tenth grade.

"My stepdad thinks I shouldn't date high-school boys until next year, but Mom says it's all right as long as the guy doesn't have a driver's license."

I didn't say anything because I knew Rachel didn't really expect an answer. She mostly wants me to listen while she tries to figure things out for herself.

"Eric is cuter than Chris, but Eric chews to-bacco," she added.

I glanced at her. Rachel is kind of plump and soft-looking, with a roundish face, but all the boys seemed to like her. Was that because of her figure, I wondered—or because Rachel was so comfortable around them?

"Did you ever kiss a guy who chews tobacco?" she asked.

As a matter of fact, I'd never kissed anyone except my parents and grandparents, but I was not about to tell Rachel that. "No," I admitted.

"Eric says it kills germs, but I—" Rachel broke off as Mr. Gembar approached.

"What are you doing?" he asked Rachel.

"Trying to make a pretty pattern."

"Listen to the wood. It'll tell you what it wants, how its grain is designed to flow."

"Okay."

"Lanie." He eyed my paddle, which was sanded down to about the size of a ruler. "What is your wood telling you?"

" 'I am getting smaller and smaller.' "

"EEIH!" came a scream from across the room.

I looked up in time to see Vinnie lurch from the saw, grabbing his right index finger in his left hand.

Mr. Gembar rushed to Vinnie, seized both his hands, and bent over them.

"Ha! Ha!" roared Vinnie. "Fooled you!"

Mr. Gembar dropped Vinnie's hands. He stared at him for a long moment, then said, "Report to me every day after school for the next two weeks. While you clean up in here, we can discuss your future behavior."

"Why not give me detention?" asked Vinnie, who is trying to establish a school record for the most detentions ever.

Mr. Gembar didn't answer.

"Isn't it illegal to force kids my age to work?"

Mr. Gembar took out his keys and locked the saw Vinnie'd been using so it wouldn't operate.

"You'll be sorry," threatened Vinnie.

"Three o'clock, this room." Mr. Gembar moved on to the next saw where he began to show Jerome how to maneuver the blade across the grain.

I began sanding again, thinking of the kids in the hall before class. Vinnie wouldn't do a thing to Mr. Gembar, because he knew Mr. Gembar was in charge in his class. As for science . . . No one was in charge in there, and anything could happen.

5

I didn't worry much about my science grade the next few days, because I had a new problem. Chris didn't come back to our table at lunch. Instead, Vinnie started sitting across from me, making stupid jokes and eating with his mouth open. He'd bite into his bologna sandwich, make a joke, then laugh, giving me the perfect opportunity to see white bread, pink bologna, and red ketchup ground together by his slimy yellow teeth. In three short days Vinnie ruined both bologna sandwiches and lunch period for me.

"Unless I leave all my friends and move to another table, I'm stuck with him," I complained to Jill as we entered my house on Friday after school. "Watching him eat practically makes me sick," I added as we took cans of pop from the refrigerator and went to my room to work on our fashion albums.

"School's what makes *me* sick," said Jill, "all the

homework and studying for tests." She sat cross-legged on the rug, her album on her lap. "I just know I failed that quiz on the earth's strata."

"It won't count much," I told her, thinking that Jill had never failed anything in her entire life.

"Everything counts," Jill observed gloomily. "Don't forget to bring your salt Monday."

"Don't worry. It's already in my purse."

"Mine too." Jill reached for one of the fashion magazines I'd collected from Sophie's room. She opened it to a full-page advertisement, then picked up the scissors. "Do you think that fits in with my style?" she asked, pointing at a tall, slender girl in an emerald blouse and a sleek black skirt.

"Sure thing," I said, since Jill wants to be a glamorous, sophisticated type. I watched her cut out the ad and place it in her album. Most of the clothes she'd selected were in blacks and greens. I picked up my own album and leafed through it.

"I'll never settle on my style," I complained. "Look at these pictures. One outfit is all lace; the next looks like I'm headed for a mud-wrestling contest."

"Let's see." Jill leaned across the magazines between us to examine the fashion album I was putting together. She flipped back several pages to display a girl in a prom dress, the skirt tiers of yellow lace with a satin top edged in the same delicate material. On the opposite page was a Three Rivers ad. It showed a healthy female in shorts, a T-shirt, and hiking boots. She was complete with backpack and had forgotten to shave her legs.

"That's Lanie," said Jill, pointing to the girl in hiking boots. "The one in lace is Melanie Anne."

"Really?" I compared the pictures. "The Three Rivers ad seems more like me. The girl in the prom gown reminds me of Rachel."

"Rachel's too fat to be a model." Jill continued flipping pages, stopping here and there to examine a selection more closely.

"I meant her face," I explained. "Besides, Rachel isn't really fat."

"The boys sure like the way she's built." Jill paused a long moment to study a photo of a model in tiger-striped tights and high orange boots. "After all, she *is* second runner-up sex symbol for the eighth grade."

"I never heard that!"

"Don't you remember? The kids voted the day before Thanksgiving. It was Greg Pucci's idea."

"That was when I was absent with strep."

"Rachel pretended she was embarrassed," said Jill, "but everyone could tell she loved it."

"Who came in first?"

"Ettie Yegli."

"Ettie must weigh three hundred pounds!"

"I guess some guys thought it was funny to vote for her."

"Who was first runner-up?"

"Andrea Balaban."

Somehow I'd known it wouldn't be me.

Jill tilted my album so I could get a good view of the girl in tiger tights. "Would you actually go out in public dressed like that?" she asked.

"I might, maybe for roller skating tomorrow night," I told her, grinning as I imagined the expressions on the other kids' faces.

"Seriously."

"Sophie does." My sister's a junior. The way she dresses reminds me of Mr. Fisher's violets, her colors bright and jewel-like.

Jill frowned at the girl in the ad. "Yeah," she said.

We went back to cutting out pictures and placing them in our albums. That's one of the things I like about Jill. We can spend hours together poring over fashion magazines or making the rounds of stores at the mall. Rachel doesn't have much time to go shopping; when she does go, it's usually with her mom.

"Rachel's been asking my advice on boys," I told Jill.

"What kind of advice?"

"Like whether to go out with Chris or with a kid in high school. The kid in high school chews tobacco."

"Yuck."

"That's what I say."

"Why'd Rachel ask you?" Jill wanted to know.

"I think she only wants me to listen, but she says I'm good at figuring things out."

"You are."

"I'd have to be to give advice on boyfriends," I said. "I've never even been asked out."

"You aren't the only one." Jill made a face. "Personally, I think you're a lot prettier than Rachel," she said. "I love the way your hair gets those light-blond streaks in the summer, and you're so tall." She sounded wistful.

"Tall is no advantage," I told her, "especially when most of the boys are shorter than I am." Then I brightened. "I get lots of information about boys from Sophie. She's had loads of dates."

"Sophie tells you about her dates?"

"No, but I'm very good at observing."

"Amy never tells me anything," said Jill. "Whatever I learn I find out from her diary."

"You read your sister's diary?"

"Don't you?"

"Of course not!" I was shocked. "I mean, a diary is private."

"Getting information from observing is practically the same as reading her diary."

It didn't seem the same to me. I studied a picture of a model in safari clothing, wondering if I'd ever get to Africa. I was about to ask Jill what she thought of the outfit when I heard the front door close. "Sophie must be home from her play rehearsal," I said. "Maybe she'll run us out to the mall."

"My mother could pick us up. She's coming for me at five anyway."

"I'll ask her." I jumped to my feet.

"Want me to gather up the magazines?"

"No, thanks. Be back in a minute."

Sounds carry in our house. I was only a few feet from my bedroom door when I realized Sophie was not alone.

"If you want to be an actress, you'll have to learn

to memorize lines fast," said a low voice. "That's what's known as being a quick study."

"I still don't think Harry would like it," responded a higher voice.

"Jill," I whispered, poking my head back into my bedroom. "Come on. Observation time."

"Which is more important, Harry or your career?" came from the living room.

"Well . . ."

"Besides, I help you to learn lines; you help me. How can Harry object to that?"

"Who's she with?" asked Jill.

"I don't know, but he's not her boyfriend."

We had to strain to hear the next sentence, because the boy was speaking more quietly. "There's a kissing scene in the third act," he said. "We can practice that."

Jill put one hand to her mouth to smother a giggle.

"I'm not even in the third scene," Sophie protested.

"No, but I am." There were some scuffling noises.

Jill and I exchanged glances, then moved down the hall, closer to the living room.

"Cut it out!" said Sophie.

"Nobody'll look at Gina while you're on stage," said the boy. "You should have the female lead."

"Talk about fast lines," said Sophie. "I'd have to be four inches shorter for that part."

I dropped to my hands and knees and crept forward to peek into the living room.

Sophie and the boy were standing by the fireplace. Sophie was wearing a turquoise shirt hanging open over a bright yellow undershirt. She had soft red suede slacks tucked into the tops of yellow boots. A loose chain belt circled her slender waist.

I didn't recognize the boy. He had short black hair and was wearing jeans and a down vest. At the moment he was murmuring something into Sophie's ear.

"You'd better go, Andrew," said Sophie, backing away from him. "I don't feel right alone here with you."

Jill edged her head around the doorway to the living room. Then she jerked back. "That's the boy my sister's after!" she hissed.

"Did you hear a noise?" asked Andrew.

"What kind of noise?" said Sophie.

"Like whispering."

"Maybe my little sister—" Rapid footsteps crossed the living room.

"Lanie!"

"We were trying to find a contact lens." Since I was wearing glasses and Jill has perfect vision, I didn't mention whose contact lens.

"Who is that?" Andrew peered over Sophie's shoulder at Jill and me.

"My sister and her friend," Sophie said as Jill and I scrambled to our feet. "Lanie and Jill, this is Andrew Mastrianni."

"Hello," I said.

"Andrew's in the play," explained Sophie. "He gave me a ride home from practice."

"We heard."

"I thought you might have."

Probably to change the subject, Jill asked Andrew, "Are you related to Anne Mastrianni?"

"She's my sister." Andrew put one arm casually around Sophie's shoulders.

"I know Anne," said Jill. "She's in most of my classes."

"That's great." Andrew looked bored. He glanced at me, then added, "I guess you know Anne too."

I nodded. "She's a neat kid," I told him.

"I'm Amy Ebert's sister," said Jill. "The cheer-leader."

"Oh," said Andrew. "Her."

Ignoring Andrew's lack of enthusiasm, Jill added, "I think Amy likes you."

Andrew looked startled, then angry. For a second I thought he would say something negative, but then he just shrugged.

I glanced at Jill, expecting her to be upset by his reaction.

Jill wasn't the least bit upset. If anything, she was pleased. When our eyes met, her lips curved into a little smile and she winked at me. "See?" she seemed to be saying. "Not everybody thinks Amy's so won-derful."

I couldn't help feeling sorry for her. I mean, here was Sophie, who at the moment looked ready to clobber me—but I'd never tell one of her secrets. As for Sophie, she truly loved me even though I'm bratty sometimes. Wasn't that the way it was sup-posed to be with sisters?

6

When I entered science class Monday, the first thing I saw was Mr. Fisher's African violets. They were curled and withered as if they'd had no water for a long time. I crossed to the windowsill to examine them.

The reddish-purple flowers were no longer jewel-like. Instead, the soft petals had dark edges. Their centers were faded like crepe paper that's been left in the sun. I reached one finger to touch a hairy leaf. It was limp.

Feeling a presence beside me, I looked up.

"Salt," Mr. Fisher explained. "Few plants can tolerate it." His voice was husky, but lacked the despair I'd become used to. He sounded almost resigned.

"I'm sorry," I said.

"Did you have anything to do with it?"

"No." Thinking of the saltshaker in my purse, I

crossed my fingers like a little kid. "They were so pretty. I liked to look at them during class."

"I've noticed."

"Your posies don't look too good," interrupted Vinnie. "Hey, guys!" he shouted. "Mr. Fisher's posies are no-sies. Get it? Noooo more."

"Sit down, Vincent," Mr. Fisher said in a tight voice.

Vinnie cocked his head at Mr. Fisher, but went to his desk.

I thought Mr. Fisher would give us a lecture about destroying other people's property, or at least mention his violets, but he didn't. When we were seated, he reached into his desk drawer and brought out the tests he'd given the previous week. He passed back the big exam on the Ice Age and waited for the moans and groans to subside. I stared at my paper. Mr. Fisher hadn't given me a zero; he'd lowered my grade instead. A large B was written at the top of the page. The B was crossed out and a smaller C entered in red beside it.

"It appears that no one was listening very carefully when I covered this material," Mr. Fisher told us, holding up the quizzes on strata. "So I'm going to do you a favor and repeat the lesson today. You'll have another exam tomorrow with the same questions."

Chad groaned and Greg burped. Jill put up her hand.

"Jill?"

"Will the grade on the first quiz count?"

"Of course."

"Sheet," said Vinnie.

Mr. Fisher turned a long look on Vinnie. "What did you say?"

"Sheet."

"Report here after school today and for the rest of the week."

"For saying 'sheet'?"

"You heard me." Mr. Fisher reached to brush the curl off his forehead.

"I can't." Vinnie grinned. "Mr. Gembar has me helping him after school this week and next."

"Then report to me the week after that."

For once Vinnie was silent. We all were.

"The various layers that comprise our planet are called strata," began Mr. Fisher in determined tones.

Jill cleared her throat, then wiped at her nose with the back of her hand. She reached into her purse for a pencil, took a blank sheet of paper, and began to make notes.

I tried to concentrate on what Mr. Fisher was saying. I even got out a pencil and paper like Jill, but my mind wouldn't cooperate. Halfway down the page it wandered. Instead of sitting in science, I was transported to the Rainbow Roller Rink and Saturday's skating party.

Following Sophie's advice, I'd worn my new orange, blue, and yellow striped top with a pair of jeans. I'd gone with Jill, but skated with practically everyone—all the girls anyway, and in groups with the guys. More boys would have come around too, if only Greg hadn't stuck with me most of the evening.

Sitting in class, I rearranged the people and events of Saturday evening. Greg became Chris, and instead of trying to get rid of him, I'd spent hours at his side, our skates singing on the smooth floor, our bodies moving like a perfectly matched pair of champion skaters.

Mentally burrowing into Sophie's closet, I dug out the high-necked black silk blouse that was her favorite and topped it with the pink feather boa she'd gotten for the school play. The pink boa floated in a long stream behind Chris and me as we skated ever faster, my long legs clad in silver tights . . .

"Lanie!" hissed Jill from across the aisle. She

coughed, then wiped her nose with the back of her hand again.

Couldn't Jill see I was busy? I frowned at her and tried to recapture my daydream.

Jill mimicked blowing her nose, then reached across the aisle to tug at my purse.

I let her take it, eyeing Mr. Fisher blankly for several seconds.

"Another important aspect of our earth's strata . . ."

Chris and I hesitated at one end of the polished floor. The rest of the crowd stopped skating to form an admiring audience. The music began.

"If the glaciers had . . ."

Behind me Anthony made a bird twitter. Mr. Fisher paused in midsentence, looked toward us, then continued to lecture as he moved across the front of the room to a place where he could see down the aisle between Jill and me.

Jill must not have been paying attention to him. She extended a slender arm across the aisle to return my purse. As I watched, part of me noted one of her fingers was caught in the shoulder strap. Another part of me struggled to relocate myself in Chris's arms.

When Jill pulled her hand away, my purse jerked,

then tumbled from the desk, turning over as it descended. I shot upright and grabbed, too late. The purse landed with a thump, spilling its contents onto the floor.

Mr. Fisher came closer.

Lipstick, combs, a wad of tissues, an old note from Rachel, two pencils, a pen, and my wallet tumbled across the green tile, but they were harmless. What caused the sudden lurch in my stomach was the sight of the saltshaker. It had rolled from my purse, leaving a white trail of salt as it went.

Anne leaned out of her seat to help me. As her fingers touched the saltshaker, she glanced at me, her blue eyes questioning.

I raised my eyes from Anne's, up and up, past gray slacks, white shirt, navy tie with red dots, into other blue eyes.

"Melanie?"

"Yes."

Mr. Fisher looked at the saltshaker, then at me.

The palms of my hands went wet at the same time my mouth went dry. I bowed my head over the mess on the floor, picking up objects with shaking fingers and jamming them into my purse. I'd always had trouble with that zipper; no wonder Jill hadn't gotten it closed.

"What's happening, man?" asked Anthony, stretching to see better.

"Did you put salt on Mr. Fisher's flowers?" asked Anne, her voice low.

"No," I said, meeting Mr. Fisher's eyes. "Honest."

"Way to go, Lanie," said Vinnie.

"I want to see you after school, Melanie," Mr. Fisher told me with a sick expression on his face.

7

If Mr. Fisher had *looked* sick, I practically *was* sick by the time last period was over. Before reporting to the science room, I stopped at my locker for cough drops, hoping to ease the dryness in my mouth and the queasiness in my stomach.

"Want me to come with you?" asked Jill, falling into step with me as I headed toward the science room.

"No, thanks."

"I'll wait for you near the entrance by the parking lot."

"I don't know how long Mr. Fisher'll keep me."

"I'll call Amy to pick us up."

I nodded.

"Remember, he doesn't have proof," Jill told me as we parted. "A lot of us brought salt."

If anything, Jill's words only made me feel worse.

A lot of us *had* brought salt, but no one else had admitted it when I got caught.

Mr. Fisher wasn't in his room. Neither were the violets. The windowsill looked very bare and slightly dirty without them.

Perhaps Mr. Fisher'd taken the violets to the office as evidence, I thought. Or he could be calling my parents. I shuddered, hoping he wouldn't do that.

When Mr. Fisher finally arrived, he sat at his desk and motioned toward the nearest student desk. "Sit down," he told me, "and explain what you were doing with salt in your purse."

"I don't know," I mumbled, reminding myself how much I hated Mr. Fisher.

"There must be a reason."

I stared at the desktop, tracing with one finger a heart that had been drawn there in ballpoint pen.

"Melanie?"

"A bunch of us kids were joking around about dumping salt on your plants," I said slowly, wishing I didn't feel so much like throwing up. "We all decided to bring salt to school today. It didn't mean anything."

"How many kids?"

I shrugged.

"The situation in your class is completely out of hand," he said, "but I don't know what I've done that a student would want to destroy my plants."

"It's what you don't do," I muttered, watching my finger trace the heart.

"What don't I do?"

"Control the class," I said resentfully. "Kids get away with murder in here."

For a few seconds Mr. Fisher didn't answer. I listened to the cheerful gurgle from the fishes' aerator and tried to hold back tears. If I was in trouble, it wasn't my fault. It was his.

"Do you have any suggestions?" he asked.

When I looked up at him, he added, "I called you in, Melanie, in part because you're a ringleader."

"No!" I blurted. "You have everything all mixed up." My lower lip trembled, and I held onto my anger so I wouldn't cry. "I'm not a ringleader!"

Mr. Fisher pushed his curl back from his forehead, then ran his fingers through his hair and across the back of his head. He considered me for a long moment, then said, "I'm sorry. I guess I shouldn't have called you that."

I could hardly believe what I was hearing. He was *apologizing* to me! "That's what I mean," I burst out.

"You make me come in here, and then you apologize. That's not the way a teacher should act!"

"How should I act?" Mr. Fisher didn't sound angry, only interested in my opinion.

"Give me detention or call my parents. Send me to the office."

There was a short silence during which I was convinced I'd gone crazy. Then Mr. Fisher asked, "Because Jill knocked your purse on the floor?"

"No, because I was carrying a saltshaker."

"There aren't any school regulations against a student carrying a saltshaker."

"Well—" I threw my hands out in exasperation, then pushed at my glasses. "Because you think I killed your plants!"

Mr. Fisher sat absolutely still, but it seemed as if there was a lot of activity going on in his brain.

While I waited for him to decide on my punishment, I remembered an operation I'd read about, on how to wire shut the mouths of people who are grossly fat. I wondered if doctors would agree to wire my mouth shut so I could never speak again.

"Did you?" was all he said.

"No." My voice came out in a whisper. "I liked your plants. I would never kill them."

51

"I believe you."

I heaved a big sigh of relief.

"But I think you should tell me who did."

Mr. Fisher knows totally nothing about kids, I decided, but for once I managed to keep my big mouth shut and not reveal this opinion. "I don't know who put salt on your plants," I said in even tones.

"Then there's no reason to keep you any longer." Mr. Fisher hesitated, as if he was about to add more, but he didn't. Instead he told me, "Thank you for coming in."

"I didn't have a choice."

"That's true, but thank you anyway."

"What did he say?" demanded Jill as soon as I met her at the parking-lot entrance.

"He thanked me for coming in." I pushed savagely at the door. I wanted to kick it, or beat on the wall with my fists, or hit someone. I didn't know exactly why, but it had to do with my talk with Mr. Fisher.

"You're kidding."

"I'm not." I spotted the Eberts' red car and headed for it. "He asked me what I thought he should do."

"Hi, Amy." Jill opened the door to the passenger's side of the front seat and slid in, leaving room for me.

"Hi. Hello, Lanie." Amy leaned forward to look at me, her head almost touching the steering wheel. Amy's small, like Jill, but her hair is more red than chestnut, and her eyes are darker. Although she's in Sophie's grade in high school, she and my sister don't run around together. Sophie hangs out with the creative types, while Amy is a cheerleader, belongs to a bunch of clubs, and manages to make the honor roll too.

"It's nice of you to come for us," I told her.

"Anything to get out of the house." Amy backed and turned. "You kids want to go to Jake's?"

"Sure!" said Jill before I could answer. "But aren't you supposed to make dinner?"

"I had to pick up my little sis." Amy's eyes met Jill's and they both smiled. "Besides, I can buy a pizza on the way home."

"Mother'll be mad."

"She'll get over it." Amy's tone was light, carefree.

I tried to envision Sophie not caring if Mom was mad at her, and couldn't.

"Who kept you?" Amy asked as she pulled from Rosemont onto Union.

"Mr. Fisher." Frustration made my voice bitter. "He wanted advice."

"From you?"

"Yes."

"What did you tell him?"

"That he lets us kids get away with murder, and that he doesn't act the way a teacher should."

"Whew!" Amy sounded impressed.

"You ought to tell your parents what happened," said Jill.

"They'd *kill* me."

"Somebody ought to complain about him to the school board."

I shifted uneasily.

"They should fire him and hire a better teacher."

"He does know a lot about science," I said slowly.

"He sure can't teach it!"

To avoid answering, I stared out the window toward Jake's. There was a group of kids near the entrance, as usual.

"He called me a ringleader, then apologized," I said, looking back at Jill. "It was awful. I feel guilty and I didn't even do anything."

"That's dumb."

Maybe it was dumb, but I still felt guilty. I

watched Amy's expert movements with the steering wheel. She eased into a parking space with only a few turns. Sophie always has to turn five or six times. Once she mashed a bumper on our van.

"It was actually my fault," said Jill, "because I couldn't get the zipper on your purse closed."

Amy checked her makeup in the rearview mirror. "See you guys later," she said, hopping out of the car. She raised a hand over her head and waved at the kids by the entrance, then hurried to join them.

"I don't have much money with me," I said, my eyes following her. I'd kind of thought Amy was going to treat us. But she'd only picked us up as an excuse to get out of making dinner, and to go to Jake's herself.

"That's all right," Jill said. "I'm going to buy you the biggest, gooiest sundae on the menu."

"I'll pay you back," I offered.

"You don't have to." Jill gave my hand a quick squeeze before sliding under the steering wheel and out the driver's side of the car. She leaned over to look back inside at me. "After all, you are my very best friend."

8

And then Mr. Fisher apologized to Lanie," said Jill. "Can you imagine? He calls her in for killing his stupid plants and ends up apologizing!"

Anne stared at Jill vacantly, then examined the contents of her cafeteria lunch: milk, sausage, roll, mashed potatoes and gravy, celery sticks, an apple, and chocolate pudding.

"He was just trying to be fair," Rachel pointed out.

"Since when?"

"Since the beginning of the school year. Besides, I notice *you* aren't afraid to go after brownie points from him."

"I don't see why you'd say that." Jill turned red.

"I saw you coming out of his room Friday after school."

"I was only checking to see if I left my notebook in there."

Rachel said, "Have it your way," as if she didn't believe Jill.

"He's so dumb, he thinks we're all on the same side," continued Jill.

"I don't see why there has to be sides," I said.

"But, Lanie . . ." Jill's eyes were enormous in her delicate face. "You're the one who said it always feels like us against him."

I was saved from answering by Chris, who put his tray down on the table opposite mine. He reached for the chair.

"Hey! That's my chair!" Vinnie threw his sack lunch almost on top of Chris's tray.

"I don't see your name on it."

"I've been sitting here practically all year."

"You have not. You were sitting with Julius Palmenter until a monitor split you up."

"It seems like all year," I muttered, but neither boy heard me. They were facing off, each with a hand on the chair between them. Although Chris was cuter than ever with his eyes flashing anger, Vinnie reminded me of a cornered rat as he cocked his head and bared yellowish teeth.

Chris could beat Vinnie easily in a fight, but we all knew Vinnie had an advantage. If Chris got into trouble at school, his parents would ground him.

Vinnie's parents probably didn't care how much trouble he was in. Besides, he might get some extra detentions, which would move him closer to the record.

Chris called Vinnie an ugly name, then picked up his tray and went to another table. Vinnie peeled off his jacket, threw it on the floor beside the chair, and sat. I hunched over my meal, stirring my chocolate pudding.

"Beethoven's last movement," said Vinnie.

I pretended not to hear that, but Vinnie didn't seem the least bit discouraged. He took a huge bite of bologna and ketchup sandwich, and chewed as he stared at me, the same as every lunchtime.

On the far side of the cafeteria, Mr. Fisher came off the food line and carried his tray into the little alcove where the teachers eat. He was followed by Mrs. Aston and G. G. Jones, a gym teacher who is also the boys' basketball coach. None of them looked happy over what was on their lunch trays.

Jill leaned closer to me and whispered, "I have to go to the girls' room. Don't let anyone take my place."

"I won't." Although most kids were already seated, I added my books to hers on the chair, then picked up my fork and dug it into my mashed potatoes. As I lifted a forkful to my mouth, I peeked from under my lashes to see if Vinnie was still watching me.

He was. "On Historical Figure Day, I'll come as the horse if you come as Lady Godiva," he said.

Lucky for me that was when the food fight erupted on the other side of the cafeteria. Otherwise I might have ended up in the office for crowning Vinnie with my tray.

Later Andy Anderson said Julius Palmenter had spit in his pudding, but Julius denied it. Chad claimed his part was a terrible accident. At the sight of Andy dumping pudding on Julius, he'd squeezed his apple so hard it slipped from his fingers. He said the fact the apple had banked off Andy's head was pure coincidence.

By the time the rest of us realized what was happening, kids at nearby tables were throwing food. I saw one boy lean over, take a big fistful of potatoes and gravy, and shove it into another boy's face. A girl dumped her milk on the girl sitting next to her.

Screams and the crash of trays accompanied the screech of chairs as other students jumped to their feet. Within seconds the entire cafeteria was in an uproar. All around me kids were climbing onto chairs and yelling, "Fight!"

"Go!" yelled Vinnie, shaking his arms like a cheerleader. "Go, Julius!"

Then G. G. Jones ran from the teachers' table, blowing his whistle. He charged into the crowd, grabbed the two biggest boys, and pushed them up against the nearest wall. He reached for Julius as Mr. Fisher, Mrs. Aston, and the monitors waded in to help him.

Although the food fight had only lasted a few minutes, it added up to trouble for a lot of people. Mrs. Aston, Mr. Fisher, G. G. Jones, and the two cafeteria monitors sorted the worst offenders out of the crowd. The monitors marched those kids out of the cafeteria in a double line.

"Did you see old Julius?" Vinnie gloated over his biggest competition in the detentions contest. "I bet he'll get suspended, maybe for the rest of the school year."

"What happened?" asked Jill, returning to her seat. "Why are they taking all those kids to the office?"

"Food fight," said Julius. "Marcu will be calling parents until midnight." Mr. Marcu is our assistant principal in charge of discipline.

It was amazing how soon lunch period was over

after that. I wouldn't have had time to finish my lunch even if I'd wanted to. It seemed Jill had just sat down, and Vinnie was still chewing bologna, when the warning bell rang. Then such a crowd formed at the waste bins that there was almost another fight.

"Will you do something for me, Lanie?" Mrs. Aston asked as I dumped my tray.

"Sure." Although she had a big smear of mashed potatoes on one sleeve of her red shirt, Mrs. Aston seemed as calm as normal, even after helping to stop the food fight.

"I have papers to return to the office, and I'd like to clean up this mess on my sleeve before my next class."

"I'll drop them off." I glanced at Mr. Fisher. "Will I need a late pass to science?"

"That's all right," he told me. "I know where you're going."

In the office I had to wait a long time before the secretary noticed me. She was busy making phone calls, checking a list in front of her before each call. The doors to both the principal's office and to Mr. Marcu's office were closed. Ms. Garfield, our school guidance counselor, had her door shut too. Chad and three other boys were sitting on a bench in the outer office. Two boys and two girls stood along the wall that was covered by the office bulletin board. One of the girls was crying.

"Mrs. Aston asked me to deliver these papers," I said to the secretary when she finally glanced at me.

She looked back at the list in front of her, then said something to the person at the other end of the line.

I thought of putting the papers on the counter and leaving, but decided the office was far more interesting than science would be.

One of the kids on the bench had mashed potatoes down the front of his shirt and a worried expression in his eyes. Next to him sat Julius, his hair stiff with pudding, and beside him a boy with a small cut on his cheek. The boy with the cut was picking at it, trying to make it bleed. Chad had his eyes closed.

I turned so I could see The Room. The Room is where students sometimes have to sit for punishment. It's tiny and bare, with no windows. The only light comes from a crack between the door and the floor.

A girl emerged from Mr. Marcu's office. She went to the counter and told the secretary, "I need a pass for class."

She nodded, then spoke again on the phone.

Mr. Marcu came out of his office. "Julius," he said.

Because Julius didn't completely close the door, I could hear every word spoken in Mr. Marcu's office.

"Suppose you tell me what happened," said Mr. Marcu.

"There was a food fight."

"What did you do?"

"Nothing. I just watched."

"Then why are you here?" asked Mr. Marcu.

"G.G. Jones grabbed me out of my chair and the monitors dragged me down here."

"What for?"

"Nothing."

"You had to do something."

"I didn't! G.G. hates me!"

There was a short silence while the secretary hung up the phone and began making out a pass. Then Mr. Marcu said, "Okay. Go on in The Room."

"Oh, no! Not that!" screeched Julius.

I glanced at the boys on the bench. Chad was grinning and the rest of them didn't look so worried.

"Go on," repeated Mr. Marcu.

"I'm innocent!" Julius shouted.

"I believe you have some papers for me," the secretary told me.

Reluctantly I handed them over and left the office.

As I approached Mr. Fisher's room, I sensed something was missing, but it wasn't until I reached the door that I realized what it was. I'd been late to science twice before. Both times I could have found the way by the noise alone, but this afternoon the room was quiet. I turned the knob, pushed the door open, and entered.

Except for Mr. Fisher's voice, there was total silence. The students sat at their desks, their eyes going from the teacher to me as I stood inside the door. The silence was so complete I should have heard the gurgling of the aerator as it purified the fish's water, but I didn't. I looked toward the tank, expecting to see bright shiny bubbles dancing and the tranquil sweep of black lace fins.

There was no happy gurgling from the aerator because the bubbles has ceased. So had the movements of the fish. They lay motionless on their sides, floating on the surface of the water.

9

The food fight made some kind of weird sense: One person throws food, and within seconds everybody's smearing pudding and mashed potatoes. The dead fish were different. Someone had killed those beautiful creatures on purpose.

Trying not to look at the aquarium, I crossed the room to my seat. Mr. Fisher's voice resumed, covering the material of the past months, reviewing for our nine-weeks' test.

I'd forgotten to close the door. The room was so quiet I could hear the sharp clicks of heels on tile, then the tinier clicks a dial lock makes as it moves beneath fingers. A locker door squeaked open, then seconds later crashed shut, metal against metal. From farther away came the spronging sound of a basketball against a backboard.

For once Jill, Anne, and I walked side by side to our next classes, instead of Anne's tagging on behind.

"It's not as if anything *really* awful happened," Jill said in depressed tones as we turned the corner into the next hallway.

"It's bad enough," I muttered, aware that all around us kids were still excited over the food fight. Only the people from our science class seemed subdued.

"I don't understand," said Anne, her voice hoarse. "How could anyone kill those beautiful fish?"

"Vinnie wanted to electrocute them," Jill pointed out. "Remember? He practically said he'd kill them, but I thought it was his idea of a joke."

When I turned to see Vinnie behind us, he hunched his shoulders and held out his hands. "Come on, you guys," he said. "Do I look like a fish murderer?"

"Yes," said Jill. "You even look like a people murderer."

"I hope they catch whoever did it," said Anne. She shot a vicious look at Vinnie. "That includes you, Vinnie Charles."

When we met Greg and some of the other boys in front of the gym, I put my books in a pile by Chris's on the floor, then wiped at my sweaty arms. "It's the heat," I complained, blowing upward to lift my hair from my wet forehead. "A person can't think right. No wonder there was a fight in the cafeteria."

"Whoever killed those fish is sick," muttered Anne.

"Did what?" asked Rachel, approaching from math.

"Killed Mr. Fisher's fish," said Vinnie. Then he laughed. "They got the wrong fish . . . er. Get it? Fisher!"

Rachel made a sound of disgust, either over the dead fish or at Vinnie's comment.

"I go fishing," said Chris, as if he was trying to decide what he thought.

"Lots of people do." Chad sounded casual, too casual.

"This is different," Anne pointed out. "Those fish were pets."

"Fish aren't pets," said Jill, "not like cats and dogs."

"They are too," said Rachel.

"Fish don't hurt the way other animals do." Chris folded his arms across his chest and shifted his feet, one foot knocking into the pile of books.

"How do you know?" I demanded.

Chris shrugged and folded his arms more tightly.

Vinnie's little eyes darted from one person in the group to another, never stopping on anybody for long. Greg merely watched.

Rachel sagged, her round face dejected. "The fish were all right before lunch," she said.

"You're sure?" asked Jill.

"Of course I'm sure! I have Mr. Fisher that period and I sit in the front row. I've spent practically every science class all year watching those fish."

"How were they when you guys got to class?" I asked Jill.

"Floating on top of the tank. The purifier was working and the aerator was pumping out bubbles, but the fish were bobbing around on the surface."

"The little catfish wasn't dead yet," said Anne. "He was jumping around like one of my kittens when she had fits." She looked confused, then burst into tears. Rachel patted her on the back.

"Someone must have killed them during lunch," I said, "while Mr. Fisher was in the cafeteria."

"Greg wasn't at lunch," Chad pointed out.

"I had to take a math test."

"The whole period?"

"Almost." Greg's green eyes shifted.

"I seen you down here," said Vinnie. "I was late for lunch and I seen you coming down the hall."

"I had to get my math book!" The expression in Greg's eyes became very intense. "Man, I wouldn't do that!"

"It's happening the way we talked about," I said slowly. "First the plants and now the fish—like we planned."

Mr. Gembar appeared at the edge of our group. "Have you people forgotten your projects are nearly due?" he asked.

I sighed as I followed him into his room. It used to be that all middle-school students had to take shop. Now we get to choose between wood shop, cooking, or a course on the environment. I wished I'd picked cooking.

"Are you going to the April Daze dance Friday?" Rachel whispered.

"I guess so. Sophie promised to drop Jill and me off. Want to come with us?"

"Thanks. Chris asked me to meet him there."

I removed my decorative paddle from my pile of books and went for some of the paint Mr. Gembar keeps in a cabinet at the front of the room. I'd sanded the daisy decorations off along with the varnish and had to repaint them.

As I shook the paints, then opened them one by one, I said, "Mary Beth wrote me a letter. She wants you to read it too. Can you come home with me after school, or do you want me to bring it tomorrow?"

"After school. Mom's getting off work early to take Ralphie to the dentist."

"I'll ask Jill if she can come too."

Rachel didn't answer. Sometimes I think she doesn't like Jill very much.

"Are you girls going to talk or are you going to work?" Mr. Gembar glared at us from the front of the room. "If I made one mistake—"

"It was when you went into teaching," finished Vinnie.

When the entire class laughed at Vinnie's joke, Mr. Gembar smiled. "You might be right, Vinnie," he said. "You just might have something there."

When we'd settled down to work, Rachel made some adjustments in the hinges of her jewelry box and I began repainting daisies. Lucky for me Mr. Gembar'd given us until the following Monday morning to turn in our projects. I figured I could apply the last two coats of varnish over the weekend.

When I met her on the bus, I asked Jill to come home with Rachel and me, but she had to practice her flute for her recital.

"Between flute practice and studying for her

nine-weeks' tests, Jill hardly has time for anything else," I complained to Rachel once we'd settled at my kitchen table, a big bowl of chips between us and Mary Beth's letter spread in front of Rachel.

"Um." Rachel bit into a chip and chewed, her eyes fixed on Mary Beth's letter.

"It seems like Jill is always trying to measure up to her big sister. How'd you like it if your sister was a cheerleader, in the honor society, president of the Pep Club, and in student senate?" I added.

"I don't have a sister."

"Well, I'm glad Sophie's a regular kid," I said.

Rachel laughed. "Sophie's no regular kid."

"You know what I mean. She makes decent grades, but she'll never be a cheerleader, and as far as I know nobody's ever suggested she run for student senate."

"Talking about me?" asked Sophie, coming into the kitchen and crossing to the table to take a chip. She was wearing a fringed leather vest, a blue denim work shirt, jeans, and high-heeled cowboy boots.

"I like your vest," said Rachel.

"I got it cheap at Reruns," Sophie told her. She flipped her mane of hair back over one shoulder. "They had a green velvet dress that'd be perfect for my character in the play, but Costumes already bought yellow material."

While Sophie made herself tea, I told her about the fish and about Vinnie's joke in Mr. Gembar's class. Rachel went back to Mary Beth's letter, eating chips as she read. When she'd finished, she replaced it in the tan envelope that had a black-and-yellow butterfly where the return address should be.

"I can't imagine Mary Beth with a boyfriend," she said.

"I can," I observed mournfully. "I'm going to be the last girl on earth asked for a date."

"A lot of boys like you," said Rachel.

"They sure keep it a secret."

"They're a little . . ." Rachel hesitated, then went on, ". . . afraid of you."

"Afraid?" I squawked. "What's to be afraid of?"

"I don't know." Suddenly Rachel became very interested in a chip in her nail polish. She started picking at it, making it bigger.

Turning from the stove where she was waiting for the water to boil, Sophie explained. "Probably whenever a boy acts as if he likes you, you either start giggling or blast him with that big mouth of yours."

"What am I supposed to do? Forget how to talk?"

"You didn't have to ask Greg if he was wearing his sister's skates Saturday night," said Rachel.

"They were white with turquoise laces!" It had turned out those skates were the only ones the rink had left that fit Greg. It also was true that right after I'd mentioned them, Greg stopped hanging around me.

"You should have pretended you didn't notice," said Sophie.

"Nobody would ask me out anyway," I said, beginning to sulk.

At that moment the phone rang. Since it was on the wall right next to the table, it almost made me jump out of my skin. I reached for the receiver, but Sophie ran to snatch it out of my hand.

"It's for me," she said, one hand over the mouthpiece. "Harry's calling to make up for the fight we had last night." She uncovered the mouthpiece and said, "Hello," then, "Just a minute, please."

"I was wrong; it's for you." Sophie held the receiver toward me. As if making a birth announcement, she added, "It's a boy!"

"A boy?"

"Maybe. At your age it's a little hard to tell."

"Say something," urged Rachel when I took the receiver and sat speechless.

"Hello," I said, and then listened with growing horror.

"Just a second." I looked up at Sophie, then at Rachel.

"Who is it?" she demanded.

I was too aghast to answer.

"Is it a boy?" asked Sophie.

"I think so," I muttered.

"Does he want a date?"

I nodded and covered the mouthpiece. "He wants me to meet him at the April Daze dance."

"Terrific!" Rachel bounced in her chair, knocking Mary Beth's letter from the table but not noticing. "I knew you'd get a date!"

I swallowed.

"So who is it?" said Sophie.

"Vinnie Charles," I told them. "Crumb of the earth."

10

Even though I refused to meet him at the dance, Vinnie still appeared at our table every noon. He didn't seem to mind when I started making sarcastic comments to him.

"Most people learn to eat with their mouths shut by the time they're three," I said.

Vinnie kept his mouth closed for thirty seconds. Then it was back to a nauseating view of partially chewed lunch.

"Give me one reason you won't go out with me," he said, picking a piece of bologna from between his front teeth with a thumbnail.

I couldn't believe any boy would say that in front of other people. Jill and Rachel simply looked at him. So did Chris, who was sitting on the other side of Rachel since Anne was absent.

"You're repulsive," I told Vinnie.

"Give me another."

"It isn't Halloween."

Vinnie laughed.

"I can't stomach food with you sitting across from me," I added, "and if I lose any more weight, my parents are going to have to buy me all new clothes."

When Vinnie laughed again, Chris stared at me with a flicker of interest in his eyes. It was the first time he'd looked directly at me since the day he'd splashed milk on my top.

Cafeteria was quiet the rest of the week, but classes were even quieter, including science. This was partly because some of us were upset over the fish, but mostly because there were fewer students present. All the kids who took part in the food fight had been suspended for two days and given ten detentions.

Vinnie only learned of the detentions on Friday when the food fighters returned to school in time for the nine-weeks' tests. "It isn't fair," he protested. "Julius didn't do anything worth ten detentions."

"That's what the rest of us got," Chad told him.

Vinnie scowled. "Some people have all the luck," he muttered. "Julius already had one advantage because he was held back last year. Now I'll never catch up before summer vacation."

"I'd give you mine, but Mr. Marcu wouldn't let me," said Chad.

"It's not as if Julius really earned them," continued Vinnie. "He just happened to be in the right place at the right time."

"If you get into big trouble, you can still beat Julius," I pointed out.

"Yeah." A dreamy expression formed on Vinnie's pinched features. "I'll have to think up something really big, really spectacular."

I couldn't help being cheered by that idea. If Vinnie got into a lot of trouble, he might get suspended. Then I wouldn't have to eat opposite him every day.

"If anybody comes up with a good idea, lay it on me," said Vinnie.

The person who thought of an idea was Jill, on the way to science from the cafeteria.

"Why don't you confess to killing Mr. Fisher's fish, Vinnie?" she said. "That should be worth four or five detentions."

Vinnie looked so surprised Jill'd actually spoken to him that I thought he'd agree. Then he said, "I want old man Marcu mad at me, not a bunch of girls."

"Don't report to Mr. Gembar this afternoon," I suggested.

"I have to. I'm almost finished with my model of the earth's strata." Mr. Gembar had let Vinnie keep the leftover wood from shop and showed him how to laminate the pieces together. Vinnie'd mounted the results on a big board, labeling them according to a diagram in our science book.

"A model like that should be worth a lot in extra credit," Jill said, as if thinking out loud.

The look Vinnie turned on her was deeply suspicious. "You want something, Jill?" he asked.

"Let me borrow it."

"You? Get real."

"I'll pay you five dollars."

As Vinnie stopped walking to consider, the crowd behind bumped into him, then pushed him on.

"Please," said Jill.

I held my breath. I knew Jill was worried about her grade in science, but I'd never guessed she'd actually pay for extra credit.

"I need extra credit myself if I'm going to pass," said Vinnie. "Besides, I'm giving it to my mom for Mother's Day."

"Maybe you aren't so repulsive, Vinnie," I blurted, then clamped one hand over my treacherous mouth. I removed the hand to say, "But I still won't go out with you."

"Convince me." Vinnie sounded happier than he'd been since discovering Julius had surged ahead in the detentions race.

I didn't have time to convince Vinnie because we'd arrived at the science room. Mr. Fisher stood by his desk, holding a stack of nine-weeks' tests. Behind him and off to one side was the empty fish tank.

That nine-weeks' test was the most difficult I'd ever taken, harder than the standardized tests we had earlier in the year. It was three pages long: fill-ins, matching, true-or-false, and an essay question. After the first fifteen minutes my hands were so sweaty I could barely hold my pencil. By the time the period ended, my head ached from trying to think of answers.

It was a good thing the dance was that evening. It was the best chance I'd get to forget about the test and how my parents were going to react when they saw my nine-weeks' science grade. If I received anything less than a C, I was certain to be grounded.

With that in mind I took extra care with my appearance that evening, curling my hair and wearing it pulled back from my face. When I'd applied blush to my high cheekbones and gloss to my lips, I stepped back to examine myself in the mirror. The indigo shirt, borrowed from Sophie, brought out the blue in my eyes, and my jeans were a perfect fit. I smiled at myself, then removed my glasses to see how I'd look with contact lenses.

My body disappeared into a smudgy blur of blues topped by a flesh-colored blob.

"Ready?" asked Sophie, appearing in the doorway.

"Ready." I shoved my glasses back into place. Then we were off to pick up Rachel and Jill.

When we arrived at school, the three of us headed straight to the girls' room to make certain our appearances hadn't degenerated in the car. I, for one, looked just the same as I had at home: long curling hair, high cheekbones, and blue eyes framed by glasses.

"Hurry up, Jill," said Rachel. "The music's started."

"Just a second." Jill was leaning over a sink to apply Big Lash to her eyelashes. She put the cap back on the Big Lash, dropped it into the large shoulder bag she was carrying, then searched the purse, coming up with a lipstick.

Rachel heaved a big sigh. Although she wore

barely any makeup, her cheeks glowed, either from excitement or in reflection of the crimson sweatshirt she was wearing.

Noticing Jill's hands were shaking, I asked, "Are you nervous?"

"A little bit."

"There's nothing to be scared of," I assured her.

"I never know what to say to boys."

"You don't have to say anything," Rachel pointed out. "Boys only want girls to listen."

"That isn't fair," I protested.

Jill ran both hands down over her chestnut hair. "I'm ready," she said.

"Cheer up," I told her as we left the rest room. "At least you won't have Vinnie hanging all over you."

"If you didn't talk to him, he'd let you alone." Jill tugged at the green sweater she was wearing over black slacks, as if trying to make it fit more loosely.

"I can't help myself. When I get mad, words pop out."

"You wanted a boy to ask you for a date," said Rachel.

"A boy; not Vinnie."

"Like who?" asked Rachel.

Jill and I glanced sideways at each other. When she winked, I had trouble smothering a giggle.

"Anybody but Vinnie," I told Rachel.

As we passed the corridor leading to the science wing, I noticed the metal gate across it was standing open. Unlike other halls, this one blazed with light. From the nearest classroom came the clank of a metal bucket. A woman wearing pale green emerged from the room to dump a wastebasket into a large sack fastened to one end of a cleaning cart.

Rachel waved at the woman, who waved back, then pulled her cart several more feet down the hall.

"That's Chris's mother," Rachel explained.

"How do you know?" I asked.

"The cleaners always take a coffee break in the teachers' lounge around nine-thirty. Last Friday night Chris and I took them doughnuts." Rachel paused inside the entrance to the gym. "Hey. The decorations are great."

The dance committee had hung green and gold crepe-paper streamers, which met in the rafters and fell in long curves to the walls. Under subdued lights yellow and green umbrellas were bright against the salmon-colored walls. In one corner pots of red tulips and yellow daffodils flanked a cluster of tables and chairs.

On the opposite side of the gym from us, in front of a sign proclaiming APRIL DAZE, was Vinnie. He was jumping, trying to grab hold of one end of a green streamer.

"The dance's barely started and already he's trying to tear down the decorations," said Jill.

A speaker made a loud squawk, then some chattering sounds. Following a brief silence music filled the gym.

"Let's dance!" shouted Rachel.

Jill shook her head.

I moved in rhythm to the music, smiling and beckoning toward Jill. Two boys began arm wrestling at a table under a basketball hoop and eight or ten others formed a huddle. A gang of seventh-grade girls deserted the gym, heading toward the rest rooms.

When Jill backed away from me, I grabbed one of her hands. "Come on, silly," I said. "Dance like we practiced."

Jill was really good at dancing, better than Rachel or me. After several minutes she relaxed, her shoulders loosened, and her body moved gracefully to the music.

Chris appeared about ten minutes later. When Rachel went to talk with him, Jill and I continued to dance. She seemed to have forgotten her shyness, and I was happy because Vinnie'd decided to ignore me. He contented himself with tearing down crepe paper and yelling crude comments at any girl who came near him.

About nine o'clock Greg showed up. He had a Walkman in the pocket of his plaid shirt, the earphones hanging around his neck. Through them came a faint sound of music.

"Hi, Lanie," said Greg.

I leaned toward Rachel and whispered, "Did you and Chris set this up?"

Rachel pretended she couldn't hear me, but Jill asked, "What are you whispering about?"

"Tell you later," I promised. Then I spotted Vinnie headed in our direction. I bent my knees, trying to hide behind Chris and Greg, but it was no use.

"Think fast!" yelled Vinnie as he threw a huge wad of green and gold crepe paper at me. He had a gold crepe-paper streamer hung around his skinny neck. "Still in love with me?"

"Get lost," I told him.

"Want to dance?" Vinnie snapped his fingers and rolled his head. He'd washed his face for the occasion and had come up with a tattered red baseball cap. The cap had the plastic figure of a girl in a red bikini pinned to the bill.

"I'm with Greg." I seized one of Greg's hands.

"You are?" Greg blinked, then grinned at Chris. "See. She *does* like me."

I winced inwardly, but a new burst of music gave me an idea of how to get farther away from Vinnie. "Let's dance," I said to Greg. I pulled him away from the group.

"Hey, Jill," said Vinnie. "I thought you were too good for a middle-school dance."

I couldn't hear Jill's reply because the music picked up volume. Besides, I had to concentrate on staying out of the way of Greg's arms, which he was throwing about strangely. At one point he placed his hands on his hips and waved his elbows like wings. Then he bent his knees and hopped up and down, his feet together.

"Bawk! Bawk!" he shouted. "Erk-a-doodle-doo!"

When the music stopped, Jill had disappeared. Fortunately, so had Vinnie. A lot of kids were still on the dance floor, but Rachel and Chris were off to one side, holding hands.

Oh, well, I thought. Greg was a definite step up from Vinnie. Besides, if I got tired of him, I could always blast him with my famous mouth.

Luckily for Greg that didn't become necessary. Before long he stopped hopping up and down like a chicken, and I actually began to have fun with him. It wasn't until the dance was almost over that I went looking for Jill.

The person I found was Vinnie, but he didn't see me. He was too busy jogging around the edge of the floor, the gold streamer still dangling from his neck. In a line behind him jogged eight other boys. Because they weren't bothering anyone else and the dance was practically over, the chaperones let them run.

Jill was nowhere in sight—not then, not when the music stopped. She wasn't in the girls' room either, nor was she waiting for Rachel and me in the hall. We'd given up and left the building when we finally found her standing near the bicycle rack.

"We were looking all over for you," I told her.

"Really?"

"Honest."

"My stomach was upset," she said. "I had to get some fresh air."

"I'm sorry I went off with Greg," I said, "but I had to get away from Vinnie."

Jill shrugged as if it didn't matter and continued to scan the parking lot as if searching for our car. In the security light her pale skin looked waxy and her dark eyes were luminous.

"I'm sorry," I repeated.

"That's all right," said Jill.

"Are you feeling better? We could go to Jake's. It's my turn to treat."

Jill shook her head. "I told my parents I'd be home right after the dance."

"You can call them."

Jill glanced at Rachel, then at me. She pressed her lips tightly together, then said, "I don't want to go to Jake's. I still don't feel good, and I want to go home."

I couldn't figure out if Jill was telling me the truth or if she was angry.

"I hope you're not mad at me," I said as we pulled up in front of her house.

"Mad?" Jill echoed. She made a funny little sound, sort of like a laugh. "Of course I'm not mad at you." She gave my hand a quick squeeze, then ran up the sidewalk to her house, her large black purse bumping against one hip.

11

Jill must have been sick the night of the dance, because she spent most of the next day in bed and only managed to get up for her flute recital Sunday. At least that's what she told me when I called Sunday evening. Then Monday morning I missed the bus and took so long in Mr. Gembar's room that I didn't see her until lunch.

Thanks to missing the bus, I ended up being the last person to turn in my project. It was almost time for the late bell when I handed Mr. Gembar my decorative paddle. He made a check in his grade book to signify he'd received it.

"Won't you know who handed in projects when you grade them?" I asked.

Mr. Gembar glanced at me over the half-glasses he wears for close work. "I used to think that," he said, "until the year one student put his name on another person's project."

"Couldn't you tell who made it anyway?"

"Let's just say it's less trouble this way."

"Okay," I agreed. Then I added, "What do you think of my paddle?" I was hoping for at least a B, maybe an A, in wood shop, to help counteract the D I'd probably receive in science.

Mr. Gembar eyed my decorative paddle, turning it over to examine the bottom side, then turning it again so the daisy pattern was on top. "The finish is better than I expected," he admitted.

"What about the rest of it?"

"Well . . ."

"Yes?"

"Let me put it this way, Lanie. Don't plan to earn a living as a carpenter."

Since it didn't seem as if Mr. Gembar was going to give out any information about my grade, I asked him for a pass to homeroom. While he wrote it, I stared out the nearest window to the parking lot.

"Mr. Fisher's going to be late," I said, watching as he approached and got into a car not far from the window. "He's acting like he's leaving instead of coming to school."

Mr. Gembar was busy signing my pass and didn't answer.

The late bell rang, outside as well as inside, the sound from the parking lot muffled by the window.

89

Mr. Fisher must have heard it, but he seemed in no hurry to return to the building.

"He locked the door," I told Mr. Gembar, "but he's still inside the car."

Although the national anthem had begun to play on the public address system, neither Mr. Gembar nor I paid any attention. He'd joined me in watching Mr. Fisher.

With the car windows rolled up and the doors securely locked, Mr. Fisher looked as if he were relaxing in the driver's seat. He put both hands behind his head, leaned back, closed his eyes briefly, and opened them again. It might have been the distance, but he looked perfectly calm.

Mr. Gembar crossed to the shop phone, which hangs on the wall next to the fire extinguisher. He lifted the receiver and spoke, then was quiet for several seconds and spoke again. After he hung up, he came back to the window. "Here's your pass," he told me, holding it out.

I took the pass and shoved it into a jeans pocket, my eyes never leaving Mr. Fisher.

On the address system Mr. Marcu was reading the announcements. Usually the principal reads them, but the principal was now crossing the parking lot to Mr. Fisher's car. He attempted to open the door on the driver's side. Then, since it was locked, he leaned over to look in the window.

"Go on to homeroom," Mr. Gembar said, but I acted as if I didn't hear him.

Mr. Fisher was ignoring the principal, instead seeming to stare back at me.

I gave a tentative wave, but he must not have noticed, because he didn't wave back. Maybe the light was reflecting off the window so he couldn't see me. Or maybe he was deep in thought about his fish, or his plants, or the animal noises.

"Get out of that car!" the principal ordered, his voice carrying in the still air. "It's eight-fifteen. The school secretary is taking your attendance."

Mr. Fisher didn't answer, but he did take his hands from behind his head. He rested them on the steering wheel.

"Mr. Fisher!" yelled the principal. He rapped on the window.

Mr. Fisher rolled down the window.

"Are you ill?"

"No," said Mr. Fisher.

"Then why aren't you in the building?"

At that point both their voices dropped and I could only catch a word here and there. I heard the principal say something about responsibility and then later mention a substitute teacher. That was when Mr. Fisher finally emerged from his car.

"I wasn't hired to baby-sit," he said loudly. "I was supposed to teach science."

"You have to . . ." the principal began. I couldn't hear what else he said because he and Mr. Fisher turned to walk toward the south entrance.

Mr. Gembar touched my shoulder. "Promise me you'll keep what we just saw between us, Lanie," he said quietly. He'd taken off his half-glasses and was holding them in one hand. His gray eyes bored into mine.

"I promise," I agreed.

Mr. Gembar put his glasses back on. "That'll be best for everyone concerned," he said.

Keeping what we had seen between us was easy. Who would I tell? Maybe Mary Beth, if she hadn't moved to Kalamazoo. If I told Rachel, she'd be upset and angry because she liked Mr. Fisher, and I didn't want to deal with her anger. Jill and the rest of the kids in my science class would probably think what had happened was funny. But it wasn't funny—not to me. It made me feel ashamed, as if it was partly my fault.

I tried to reassure myself that what I'd seen couldn't possibly have anything to do with me. After all, I hadn't asked Mr. Fisher to be a science teacher. It wasn't up to me to help him control our class.

"Yeah, but you didn't have to make things worse," insisted one part of my mind.

I told my mind to shut up.

As the morning wore on and period followed period to lunch, I brooded over it, and I knew Mr. Gembar was right. We should keep what we saw between us. Besides, I'd promised.

There was a tension that day in the cafeteria, tension like the kind that occurs before a big sports event or a thunderstorm. The clatter of trays became louder, the students more restless, more lively and talkative than normal.

Usually at such times I'm as jumpy as anybody, my mouth running and my body twitching in my seat. That day I felt strangely quiet, almost depressed, separate from what was going on around me. I noted that Vinnie didn't sit across the table; Greg was sitting in Vinnie's place, and Greg ate with his mouth shut. Chris had taken Anne's seat, and Anne had moved farther down the table. Jill seemed completely recovered from her upset stomach.

What was most different was that all this didn't seem important. What was important was the scene in the parking lot: Mr. Fisher in his car with the windows rolled up and the doors locked; Mr. Fisher saying he wasn't hired to baby-sit, but to teach science.

"What are you thinking about?" Jill asked on the way to sixth period. "You hardly said a word during lunch."

"Science."

"Are you worried about your grade?"

I shook my head, then asked, "Are you?"

"Why should I worry? I *always* get A's."

As it turned out, neither of us needed to worry. Nobody did except for Mr. Fisher. When we entered science class, he was standing at the front of the room, leaning against his desk, his arms crossed across his chest. He watched us sit down, but he didn't say anything, not until the students noticed how quiet he was and became quiet too.

"I'm going to give back your nine-weeks' test," he said, "but I don't have your grades averaged."

"Boo hoo," said Vinnie. A bird twittered near the hall door.

As if there'd been no interruption, Mr. Fisher continued, "Someone in here—and I'm certain it was in here rather than in one of my other classes— killed my plants and my fish. Such behavior is in-

94

excusable, but since it was aimed at me alone, I did not report these incidents to the office."

As he paused, I glanced at the fish tank, then at the bare windowsill. When I looked back at Mr. Fisher, he was standing erect with his hands at his sides. "This latest episode is something I can't restrict to this room," he said. "One of you removed my grade book from my desk Friday after school or over the weekend. Without that book I can't turn in grades for any of my classes this marking period."

He ignored the cheer from Vinnie, as did most of us.

"This is the theft of something that is significant not only for me, but for every one of you," Mr. Fisher told us. "You have a right to the grade you earned, and your parents have a right to know about your progress this marking period. Without a record of your work I can't provide this information."

He paused, then added, "I'm leaving this room unlocked until tomorrow morning so that whoever took the grade book can return it. No questions will be asked. If the book is not on my desk by morning, I will be forced to notify the office that it has been stolen."

12

No one turned in the grade book. Tuesday during sixth period each of us was called to the office to talk to Mr. Marcu, but the thief didn't confess. When we received our grade sheets Friday, there was a large I where our science grade should have been. The I was supposed to mean incomplete, but for me it stood for inexcusable.

"Such behavior is inexcusable," Mr. Fisher had said. Deep inside I had to admit he was right.

"Mr. Fisher thinks stealing the grade book is worse than killing the fish because it affects all of us," I told Sophie on Saturday after dinner. "But every time I see that empty aquarium, I feel sick inside."

"Maybe the person who did it didn't know any better," said Sophie. We were in her room, where she was gathering clothes and cosmetics for after the play. Since it was the evening of the second and final performance, the cast party was that night, and Sophie didn't want to come home to change clothes. She stuffed a short white skirt and a pair of red hose into the backpack she was using for a carrying case. "Some people don't understand the difference between what they want and what's right."

"The fish are dead either way," I pointed out. I pulled my legs up under my chin and dug a fingernail into a hole fraying in the cover of Sophie's orange beanbag chair. "What I can't figure out is how somebody got in to steal the grade book."

"Maybe Mr. Fisher forgot to lock his door."

"No way," I said. But he *could* have forgotten, I thought morosely, or just not bothered to lock the door. Mr. Fisher didn't seem to understand the lengths some kids might go to.

Sophie blew out her cheeks, then let the air gradually escape as she scanned the surface of her dresser. "I'm off!" she said, picking up the loaded backpack.

"We'll be clapping for you," I told her.

"Thanks." She flashed her wide smile. "I guess I won't see you until tomorrow. Have fun sleeping over at Jill's."

"I will." I watched Sophie's long, lean form disappear around the doorframe, then unfolded from the beanbag and went to my own room to dress.

That night I wore the silky purple blouse Sophie'd given me for my birthday. Mom had protested that the blouse was too old for me; but when I put it on with my straight navy skirt, hose and heels, then peered into the full-length mirror on my closet door, I decided I'd grown into it. I piled my hair high on my head, using combs to hold it in place, and added long dangling silver earrings to my ears. The result made me look much older—at least fifteen.

I might have been my most attractive, but as I watched Sophie in the play that night, I realized I'd never be in her league. She moved across the stage with the same confidence and magnetism she always had, but she seemed to have become a totally different person. On stage she was no longer Sophie; she was the glamorous sister of a famous man.

"Aren't you jealous?" asked Jill when my parents had dropped us off at her house. "Don't you just hate her?"

"Hate her?" I repeated. I couldn't imagine anyone hating Sophie.

"She's so beautiful and talented, and you're . . ."

"Big-mouthed, ordinary Lanie."

"Not ordinary." Jill eyed me. "But don't you hate all the attention she gets?"

"The fact is I get plenty of attention," I said,

recalling for a brief instant the time I'd received a D in math. "Just because my parents don't hang over me every minute doesn't mean they don't care where I go or what I do." Like now, I thought. It was fine that I was sleeping over at Jill's house. What might not be fine was if Mom and Dad found out Jill's parents wouldn't be home until very late.

"Well sometimes I hate Amy!" burst out Jill. "All I ever hear is 'Amy, Amy, Amy.' How popular precious Amy is, how she's in all those activities, where she'll go to college."

I didn't know what to say. I wasn't certain just how popular Amy was. I knew I didn't like her, but I hardly could tell Jill that. After all, Amy was Jill's sister.

"I know!" said Jill. "Let's read her diary."

"No," I said. "I don't want to."

"Don't be Miss Priss. Nobody's home, so we can't get caught. Besides, I want to find out what happened to the fight she's having with Lisa."

"She'll kill us if she finds out," I muttered, following Jill into Amy's room.

"She shouldn't leave her diary lying around where it's easy to pick up."

The diary wasn't exactly lying around. As I grew

increasingly uneasy, Jill searched Amy's dresser drawers, her desk, and under the bed. She finally located the diary in a shoe box in the closet.

"She's getting sneaky," said Jill as we returned to her room. "Sit down. I'll read it to you."

I sat down and tried not to listen, but that was impossible, especially when Jill came to the part about Amy's big date with Keith Randall. Amy and Keith went to a party where the recreation-room floor was covered with sand and cans of beer cooled in a tub in the fireplace.

"Listen to this!" Jill was saying when the front door slammed. There were running footsteps in the hall, and then the door to Amy's room jerked open. Seconds later came an enraged shout.

"Jill!"

Jill threw down the diary, jumped to her feet, and ran from the room in time to intercept Amy in the hall.

"What did you do with my keys?" demanded Amy.

"I don't have them."

"Yes you do. You borrowed them to get into the house because you lost yours. I want them back."

"Why?" asked Jill. "There'll be someone home the rest of the night."

"My car keys are on that ring. Keith's dad won't let him use their car, and we want to go to the cast party."

"What'd you do for the play?" I asked, joining them. Maybe Amy'd worked on the set or on publicity.

"Nothing." Amy narrowed her eyes at me. "Everyone goes to the cast party."

That wasn't what Sophie had told me, but for once I managed to keep my mouth shut.

"They must be in your room." When Amy tried to pass Jill, Jill stepped in front of her.

"I put them on your desk," she said.

As Amy turned and went back into her room, Jill whispered, "Hide the diary," and ran after her.

Spurred by the sound of bickering, I rapidly settled on hiding the diary in Jill's bookcase. I shoved it behind a row of paperbacks, then pulled a large book of maps from the bottom shelf.

I wasn't much interested in maps, but I needed an excuse not to face Amy when she came storming back to Jill's room. From the approaching voices, that was going to be any second. I flipped the oversized book open to what I figured was the biggest map, folded into sections to make a crack between pages.

What appeared was a red rectangle with gold lettering. Inside what should have been the last volume anyone would remove from her bookcase, Jill had hidden Mr. Fisher's grade book.

13

here they are!" Amy rushed into the room. As she pounced on the keys lying on Jill's dresser, I shut the book of maps.

"I was certain I put them on your desk," said Jill.

"See you guys around noon." Amy tossed the keys into the air and caught them as she left.

"Is she going to stay out until noon tomorrow?" I asked.

"That's just her way of warning us not to make any noise in the morning," said Jill. She crossed to me, took the book from my hands, and shoved it into the empty space on the bottom shelf. "That's just a dumb book my parents gave me. If you want something to look at, I can go get Amy's latest copy of *Vogue*."

Without waiting for an answer, she threw herself on her bed. "That was close! Where'd you hide the diary?"

"Behind the paperbacks on the top shelf."

"Get it, will you? I can't wait to find out what else happened at the party."

As I shifted other books to reach the diary, I realized that whatever I did in the next few minutes was going to affect me for a long time. If I acted as if I hadn't seen the grade book, then I wouldn't have to confront Jill with it. She and I could go on being best friends. We'd giggle together at school, go on expeditions to the mall, and work on our fashion albums and trade secrets on lazy afternoons.

But nothing could ever erase the fact I *had* seen the grade book. No matter how much I wanted those few moments not to have happened, they had. I handed the diary to Jill, then returned to stand near the bookcase as she searched for her place.

"Here we are." Jill's eyes scanned the page.

Maybe I'd been wrong from the beginning. Maybe all along Jill wasn't the person I'd thought she was—or wanted her to be. I rubbed at my forehead.

" 'About midnight Keith decided no beach party was complete without roasting hot dogs over an open fire,' " read Jill.

I bent to pull the volume of maps from the bottom shelf.

"What are you doing?" Jill lowered the diary.

I flipped past the introductory section to remove the red grade book.

"Give me that!" In one swift motion Jill dropped the diary, jumped from the bed, and crossed the room.

"No." I held it against my chest, pushing at my glasses with my free hand. "You took it."

Jill didn't answer. She only watched me.

"When?" I asked, feeling my way along.

"During the dance," she said lightly, as if it weren't of any importance. "While you were dancing with Greg and the cleaners were on break." She smiled confidentially. "You should have seen me! I was so scared!"

"But *why* did you take it?"

"Come on, Lanie," she said. "You know why. Besides, I only did what plenty of other kids wanted to do."

"You have to give it back."

"Oh, sure." Jill flung herself onto the bed and leaned back against the headboard, her arms crossed. "What do you suggest? That I tell Mr. Fisher I found it in a ditch on the way to school? Or maybe that the tooth fairy left it under my pillow?"

"But what about our grades?"

When Jill tossed her head, her chestnut hair flew

around her delicate face, then settled neatly into place once more. "Mr. Fisher'll have to give us the same grades as last marking period. Amy told me that happened once when her algebra teacher lost his grades."

"That's not fair."

"Pop quizzes aren't fair. Neither was our nine-weeks' test."

I wasn't certain about the quizzes, but the test sure wasn't fair.

"Give me the grade book and forget you saw it," Jill said in wheedling tones. "I'll get an A this marking period; you'll get a C. After a couple more months we'll never see Mr. Fisher again."

"With my luck he'll get switched to high school," I muttered. "I'll end up in his class again next year."

"Are you kidding?" Jill's large dark eyes were amused. "If you were running the schools, would you keep a teacher like him?" She paused, then added with contempt, "A nerd who can't control a bunch of eighth graders? Who loses his grade book?"

I shifted uncomfortably.

"No way will they hire him back," she told me. "Not after this."

"You're trying to get Mr. Fisher fired," I said, expecting her to deny it.

Instead, Jill smiled.

"Because of a B on your report card?"

"I'm doing everybody a favor by bringing him to the principal's attention. He's a terrible teacher."

"It still isn't right," I said, but I was weakening. The truth was that Mr. Fisher *was* a terrible teacher—at least in our class. I glanced at the red grade book. "I just wish I hadn't found the stupid thing."

"Serves you right for snooping."

"I wasn't snooping!" Jill was trying to make the whole thing seem as if it were all my fault! I bit my bottom lip, wishing Jill had never told me to hide her sister's diary, that I'd never picked up the book of maps.

Then I had a terrible thought, so terrible I couldn't keep it to myself. "Did you kill the fish?" I asked.

"No." Jill's eyes narrowed. "Vinnie did."

She was lying. Deep inside I knew it. My mind went back to the day of the food fight, and I could see Jill's empty seat beside me. She'd killed the fish and tried to throw the blame on Vinnie.

I thought back further—to the dead plants, the saltshaker in my purse, and Jill's knocking my open purse off my desk. Was there some reason Mr. Fisher might have suspected Jill of putting salt on his plants?

And did she spill my purse on purpose, to throw the blame on me?

"You made it look like I killed the violets," I said.

Jill stared at me. Then she shook her head.

"Did Mr. Fisher catch you in his room that morning?" I asked. Then, as the memory came into my mind, I added slowly, "Or the Friday before? Rachel said she saw you coming out of his room after school that afternoon, that she figured you were going after brownie points from him." I took a deep breath and went on, "And you were late to the bus. You almost missed it."

"Believe whatever you want." Jill's words were clipped, full of anger. Her lips made a tight, hard line. She shifted her eyes toward the window as if she couldn't bear the sight of me. Then, as I watched, she seemed to make up her mind about something. "If you want to think I'd do that to my best friend," she said, "I can't change your mind."

I looked silently at the pretty girl on the bed, and I felt like crying. Jill had said I was her best friend. Maybe she was my friend, but she was also my enemy.

"I don't want to believe that." The lump in my

throat made my voice a painful whisper. "I don't want to think about it at all."

"You don't have to." Jill smiled at me as if everything were settled and reached for the diary. "Do you want to hear more about the party?"

"Actually, no."

Jill stopped moving.

"Not until you promise to return the grade book."

"I can't."

"You have to."

"I do not."

"Then I will."

Jill blinked, glanced at the diary, and then looked up at me. "Are you going to tell Mr. Fisher I took it?" she asked.

"I don't know yet."

We stayed like that for a long moment, Jill on the bed and me across the room from her. The distance wasn't very great, just a few feet of bedroom carpet, but there seemed to be miles of space between us.

14

The rest of the night at Jill's is not something I like to think about. There were no more arguments between us. There was nothing at all except that invisible space with me on one side and Jill on the other. The grade book stayed where I'd put it in the inside pocket of my bag, but I felt as if it hung suspended before my face all the long hours of the night.

Like small children we watched cartoons on television in the morning until my mother came to pick me up.

"Have a good time?" asked Sophie as I carried my overnight bag into the house.

"She isn't talking," said Mom. "I don't think those girls slept a minute."

I escaped to my bedroom, cuddled up with my old Raggedy Ann doll, and slept until the middle of the afternoon. When I first awoke, I thought I'd had a nightmare, but the rectangular shape in my overnight case was all too real. I took the grade book out and stared at it, then transferred it to my blue backpack, as if by putting it out of sight I could put it out of my mind.

Knowing that was impossible, I went to find Sophie, but she'd gone to the high school to help take down the set. If I told Mom or Dad what had happened, they might make me go to the principal and reveal the whole thing. I didn't want to do that.

To make everything worse, I was confused about what had happened and the events leading up to it. I'd thought I hated Mr. Fisher, but now I wasn't so sure. I had considered him my enemy and Jill my friend—but I'd been wrong about that too.

Outside, the day was beautiful, the sky a clear blue, the air fresh with spring. Yellow flowers pushed between long green daffodil leaves, and the buds on the maples had grown fat and red. Planning a long ride alone, I took my bicycle from the garage. Instead, I headed for Rachel's.

Rachel was baby-sitting her brother Ralphie again, but at age nine, he only needed her there in case of an emergency. He was in the backyard, playing ball with his friends. Rachel was perched on the top step to the Porters' porch. She had the sleeves of her sweatshirt pushed up to expose part of her arms to the sun. It was the same sweatshirt she'd worn to the dance, but now Rachel was wearing a matching scarf tied around her black curls.

Because the front yard was mostly bare areas of mud broken by a straggly forsythia bush, I parked my bike on the sidewalk. Then I went to sit beside Rachel.

"Did you have fun last night?" she asked.

"It was okay. Want to go on a bike ride after your parents get home?"

"Chris is coming over."

"What about after dinner?"

"Chris has ten dollars left from his birthday. If he can raise some more, we're going to a movie."

"Oh." I wondered why Rachel didn't pay her own way to the movie, but she probably didn't make much money baby-sitting Ralphie. She didn't get an allowance either.

As if she'd read my mind, Rachel said, "Personally, I'd rather stay here and watch television. All Chris wants to see is movies about men with big muscles blowing people up."

"I don't know if I want a boyfriend," I told her, "especially if they only like dumb movies."

Loud shouts erupted in the backyard. Then Ralphie charged around one corner of the house, slipped in a patch of mud, and slid under the for-sythia bush.

Rachel watched him emerge on his hands and knees, pick up the baseball he'd been chasing, and disappear behind the house again. Then she said, "It's part of the deal."

"Some deal." I made a sour face. "Listen, Rachel. I need your advice."

"On boys?"

"On something more important."

Rachel looked as if she didn't think there could be anything more important.

"It's about a girl I know," I said hurriedly, before I could lose courage. "I think she did something really mean to me, but there's no proof. I can't de-cide whether I'm wrong and she's innocent or not."

"Jill."

"I didn't say who." I could feel my cheeks getting hot.

"You didn't need to."

"Anyway, maybe I should act like nothing ever happened."

"Maybe," Rachel conceded. "On the other hand this girl could make a habit of doing mean things to people, and she's only now getting around to you."

"It isn't that simple," I protested, a little bit angry because Rachel wouldn't say what I wanted to hear.

"All I can tell you is that it's nice to know who your friends are."

"I guess so," I said to be agreeable. "Thanks."

"You're welcome." Rachel smiled. "I thought maybe you were going to ask my advice on Greg."

"I only danced with him at April Daze to get rid of Vinnie."

"He's telling everybody you're going together."

"Oh no," I groaned. Then, remembering the fun I'd had at the dance, I added, "It wouldn't be so bad if he didn't go around making chicken noises."

"If you want somebody perfect, you'll never have a boyfriend."

"I don't want to talk about it," I told her. "I'd better be getting on home anyway. Nobody knows where I am."

As Rachel walked with me to my bicycle, she said, "Chris and I might come over later."

"See you then."

I went in the direction of my house, but I didn't go straight there. Instead I rode several miles, around the mini-park not far from Rachel's house, then over past Oakway Elementary, all the while thinking about the grade book. By the time I turned toward home, I'd decided what I was going to do with it.

As I rode up in front of our house, Sophie appeared from the direction of the garage with Harry and Andrew. Sophie was carrying the chains to the porch swing while the boys followed her, carrying the swing itself. Harry, who is four inches taller than Sophie and a star wrestler, strode along easily, holding his end of the swing with one hand.

Andrew is more Sophie's size. He didn't look very happy as he carried his end of the swing. He looked as if he were on some sort of death march.

"Hi, Lanie," said Sophie as they passed me on the way to the front steps.

"Hi," echoed Harry.

Andrew didn't say anything. He must have been saving his breath for the climb up the steps.

"After we hang the swing," said Sophie, "we can use it like part of a set. How many scripts did you bring, Andrew?"

"Two." He set his end of the swing down with a grunt. "What is this made of? Lead?"

"Oak. Mom ordered it special since a normal swing looked too small on our porch."

As Andrew stretched, then shifted to ease his

back muscles, it occurred to me that both Andrew and Harry seemed like nice guys—but neither one was perfect. As a matter of fact, neither was I.

"What's this about scripts?" asked Harry.

"Andrew told me The Players Guild is casting *Summer and Smoke* next Saturday," said Sophie. "He thinks I'd be terrific as the female lead."

"And this afternoon would be a terrific time for you two to rehearse," Harry observed somewhat grimly.

"What a wonderful idea!" said Sophie.

I missed what Harry said next, because I saw Rachel and Chris crossing the street two houses down the block. Greg was with them.

"Harry is the sweetest, most understanding guy I've ever gone with," said Sophie, I guess to Andrew. I didn't really care. I was on my way to meet the other kids.

"Me and Chris have a bet," Greg announced when we were close enough to talk. "I told him you're my girlfriend, but he doesn't believe me."

"Chris is right," I said, feeling a stab of remorse when Greg looked hurt.

"Then why'd you say you were with me at the dance? How come we sit across from each other at lunch?" he asked. There were little speckles of brown in his green eyes.

"To get rid of Vinnie," I explained, wishing I didn't have to admit it. Greg was a nice kid and he liked me.

"Oh."

"Pay up, man!" As he punched Greg on one arm, Chris gave a hoot of laughter. "You owe me five dollars."

No way, I thought. That just isn't fair.

"But you are kind of cute," I told Greg. "I think maybe I am your girlfriend after all."

15

Greg and I spent the five dollars I'd saved him, the five dollars he'd won from Chris, plus all his allowance, at the movies that evening. It was my first date. Because I was thinking that Greg might kiss me good night afterward, I could hardly keep my mind on the film. I kept daydreaming about my first kiss and wiping the sweat off the palms of my hands on my jeans.

The sweat and the daydreams were a waste. After Greg walked me to the door, he punched me on the arm the way Chris had punched him earlier.

"See ya around," said Greg. He sauntered down the walk to the car where his mother waited, pretending to fiddle with the radio controls, but secretly watching Greg and me.

I didn't sleep well that night because of a recurring dream. In the dream Greg was hanging around our front porch, trying to get up the nerve to kiss me. A big red grade book lurked in a dark corner of the porch. The grade book had legs and sharp teeth. It was waiting for me to concentrate on Greg so it could sneak up on me.

Normally I would have spent the time while I dressed and ate breakfast reworking my dream to make it end the way I wanted. But that morning I couldn't think of anything but returning the grade book to Mr. Fisher. I finally decided to give it to him following last period, since that was my best chance to see him alone.

Unfortunately, turning over the grade book after school meant that I was forced to carry it around all day. The first few classes I was jumpy, suspecting that Mr. Marcu would appear any second and demand I hand over my backpack, or that some kid would search it for a pencil. After that I mostly worried over what to expect from Jill during lunch. If anything I became more nervous over *her* reaction than Mr. Fisher's.

Hoping to be in place when Jill arrived, I hurried to reach the cafeteria early, but we approached the table at the same time.

"Hello, Lanie," said Jill.

"Hi."

"Did you see that lime gelatin with cherries in it?" She wrinkled her nose. "Gross."

"Mom packed me a sandwich," I told her, wondering how Jill had gone through the cafeteria line so quickly.

"Hi, Rachel. Hi, Greg," Jill said, putting her tray on the table and sitting.

Not knowing what else to do, I sat beside her. While I nibbled my sandwich, I listened to the talk at the table. When Greg mentioned something about the movie, Jill turned her big brown eyes on me.

"You and Greg went to the movies last night?" she said. "You didn't tell me."

"It was a surprise," I said. If Saturday night had never happened, I'd have called Jill the minute I found out I had a date.

"Did you have a good time?"

"Yes," I answered, knowing in that instant I was never going to tell Jill how my palms had sweated and how I'd thought Greg would kiss me, but how he'd punched me on the arm instead. "It was the new science-fiction movie at the mall," I added cautiously, as if that were revealing too much.

By then Chris had arrived. Greg began telling him about the movie, which showed future humans living in sealed capsules on Jupiter. The humans only returned to earth to mine salt, which they traded to aliens for water. "Man, you should have seen those aliens eat salt!" said Greg. He shook his head in amazement.

Personally, I hadn't liked the movie much, but I didn't say so since Greg had paid for me to see it. Besides, my mind was busy with images of the grade book and the dead fish, and with the fact that Jill was sitting next to me as if nothing had ever happened. There ought to be *something* I could do. . . .

"What do you think, Lanie?" asked Rachel, probably wanting to know my opinion of the movie.

"I think," I said slowly, "that we ought to take up a collection and buy Mr. Fisher some new fish."

There was total silence at our table. Nobody said anything and nobody moved. One of the monitors glanced in our direction.

"That's a great idea!" said Rachel.

"It is not!" said Jill. "Mr. Fisher—"

I looked at her.

She dropped her gaze and said, "If you really want to . . ."

"I spent all *my* money last night," Greg pointed out. Chris didn't say anything, but farther down the table Anne said, "Pet Party just got a new shipment of angelfish." After that everyone seemed to talk at once, at least until the warning bell rang.

"Spread the word," I told the other kids as I

cleaned up the remains from my lunch. "Anyone who wants to contribute should give me their money by Friday. I'll buy the fish over the weekend."

Jill, Greg, and I walked together to science. As I slid into my seat, Jill leaned across the aisle. Her eyes were glistening with pleasure as she whispered, "I didn't want to tell you in front of anyone else, but Amy is in big trouble. My parents found out about the party with the sand in the recreation room and the beer in the fireplace."

Jill didn't have time to say more. The bell rang, class began, and she gave her full attention to the teacher. Most of us did. After the grade book was stolen, Mr. Marcu had made a habit of dropping by Mr. Fisher's room unexpectedly. Other times we'd hear a faint click, then feel the hollow sensation caused when someone in the office listened in on our class over the intercom.

I didn't mind when sixth period was over. Although it meant my meeting with Mr. Fisher was closer, I was glad for the chance to get away from Jill. On the way to shop I just listened while she described the play to Anne and told her how lucky I was to have Sophie for a sister instead of Amy.

In shop Mr. Gembar went over the list of materials we'd need for our next project. It seemed no time at all until class was over and the dismissal bell was ringing. I went to my locker first, then slowly walked back to the science room, killing time until the halls were empty.

Mr. Fisher was alone. He'd moved the aquarium to a bottom shelf and was wiping the place where it had stood with a paper towel. When I came into the room, he crumpled the towel into a ball and pitched it into the wastebasket.

"Hello, Melanie," he said.

"Hello, Mr. Fisher." I crossed the room, my backpack heavy on my shoulder. "What are you doing?"

"Cleaning up a little. Did you want to see me about something?"

I lowered the pack from my shoulder onto the nearest desk. "This," I said, pulling out the grade book and handing it to him.

Mr. Fisher flipped quickly through the pages, as if to make certain they were all there. "Did you take it?" he asked.

"No."

I wasn't certain Mr. Fisher really believed me, but he only said, "Do you know who did?"

I nodded. "But I'm not going to tell." Mr. Marcu could put me in The Room for an entire day, but I had made up my mind that I'd never tell—not even if he put me in there forever. I stared at the grade book. "I hope you didn't lose your job because somebody took it," I said to Mr. Fisher.

"I had next year's contract before the grade book disappeared."

"You did?"

"But I hadn't signed it. I still haven't."

"Why not?"

"I'm not certain teaching is right for me."

When I didn't say anything, Mr. Fisher gave me a long, considering look. Then he put the grade book on his desk, resting one hand on it. "You know, Melanie," he said, "I had a strange experience the morning I discovered my grade book was missing. I went back to my car to check that I hadn't meant to take it home on Friday, that it hadn't slipped under a seat by mistake. After I searched the car, I just couldn't force myself to return to the building." He smiled, as if he were amused at himself, but a little embarrassed too. "I sat in my car thinking. I might have sat there the entire day if the principal hadn't come for me."

"What were you thinking about?"

"How I'd always wanted to teach, and how I've tried it, and I'm not very good at it."

Although I only shifted my feet, I felt as if every

muscle in my body jumped, as if every nerve had been touched and was tingling. Then I thought: He's doing it again—acting as if we're friends, equals.

"Rachel says you're pretty good in her class," I told him.

"Not good enough." He glanced at the empty aquarium, then at the bulletin board, where he had placed a poster of the life cycle of butterflies.

Mr. Fisher wasn't blaming us; he was blaming himself.

"It wasn't all your fault," I said tentatively.

"Maybe." He didn't sound convinced.

"If you tried again, you'd be better next year," I told him. "I know you would."

As Mr. Fisher looked back at me, I wondered if not too long ago he'd been like Greg or Chris, or like me, worrying what it would be like to go on a first date, what it would be like to kiss someone.

"I'm not certain I want to try again," he said.

There was a short silence, as if neither of us knew what to say. Then Mr. Fisher said, "Thank you for returning my grade book, Melanie. It's one of the good things that happened this year."

I could have told Mr. Fisher that I'd brought the grade book back more for me than for him, but I didn't. I only said, "You're welcome."

16

A lot of kids seemed to think it was a good idea to replace Mr. Fisher's fish. Unfortunately most of them didn't think the idea was good enough to give money toward, or else—like Greg—they'd spent all their money on other things. Rachel gave me two dollars. Anne, Chris, Anthony, and two girls I don't know very well gave me dollar bills. Other kids from our science class came up with stray dimes and quarters.

Chad Jeffers wanted to know if I'd take an IOU.

"For how much?" I asked.

"Fifty cents," he told me, then snorted through his nose. He'd been out of practice lately thanks to Mr. Marcu's spending so much time in our science class.

During lunch Friday Jill took a five-dollar bill from her purse and handed it to me. "Here," she said. "This should help you out."

Help me out! Trying to contain the anger that swept through me, I took a deep breath. Jill should be paying to replace all the fish! Instead she was making a big show of giving me five dollars toward new ones!

"Gee, Jill," said Chris. "I thought you didn't like Mr. Fisher."

"I don't," Jill told him. "But Lanie's my best friend, so naturally I've got to give *something*."

I wanted to yell, "Don't call me your best friend!" But I just pressed my lips tightly together. As I took the five dollars, I swallowed hard and managed to say, "Thank you."

I must have sounded strange, because Chris frowned and Greg gave me a funny look. Luckily at that moment Vinnie stopped by our table. "You still want donations for the fish tank?" he asked, his hands stuffed into his jeans pockets, his beady little eyes fixed on me.

"Sure," I said, wondering what Vinnie was up to.

"Here." He pulled his right hand from his pocket and held it out, fist closed, over the table.

When he realized I wasn't going to put my hand under his to take what he was holding, Vinnie turned his fist over and opened his fingers. Sitting on his palm was a tiny ceramic treasure chest. The chest's lid stood open, revealing miniature coins and jewels, a pearl necklace and a golden goblet.

"It's a decoration," Vinnie announced proudly. "I got it at my neighbor's garage sale."

"That is *so* tacky," said Jill.

"I think it's pretty," Anne protested.

"So do I," I said. "It'll look great on the bottom of the aquarium. Thanks, Vinnie!"

"Wasn't nothing." Vinnie hunched his shoulders as if he was embarrassed. Then he walked away, whistling.

"I think Vinnie has some nerve," said Jill, "after all the trouble he's caused in Mr. Fisher's room."

"He doesn't have as much nerve as some people," I told her. If Jill said one more thing about Vinnie, I was going to add that he hadn't caused nearly the trouble as some people had either.

But Jill didn't. She must have realized she'd gone too far, because she mumbled something about Vinnie not being such a bad kid.

Although Sophie had agreed to take me shopping at Pet Party Sunday afternoon, I had to arrange for a way to get into Mr. Fisher's room to set up the aquarium. No problem, I told myself. Mr. Gembar was a good guy. He'd let me in. Besides, ever since the morning we'd watched Mr. Fisher and the principal in the parking lot, Mr. Gembar had been acting like Mr. Fisher's friend. I'd seen him talking with Mr. Fisher before school in the mornings and once in the parking lot after dismissal.

"I need somewhere to keep the fish and bottled water until lunch time," I told him, "and a pass from the cafeteria, and somebody to get a key from the office to unlock the door to the science room."

"You don't need much," Mr. Gembar observed. "Why not put the fish in the tank before school in the morning?"

"Because I want Mr. Fisher to know our class bought them. Please, Mr. Gembar!"

When Mr. Gembar grinned, his gray eyes smiled too. "All right, Lanie. Bring the fish and water to the shop before school Monday morning. I'll see what I can do."

At that point I figured Mr. Gembar would more than *see* what he could do; he would do it—and I was right. Not only did he store my purchases for me Monday morning and let me into the room, but he also arranged my pass from the cafeteria, unlocked the door for me, and helped me install the fish in their new home.

"It's absolutely beautiful," I said out loud when

the aquarium was completely set up. Pet Party had only had one black lace angel. I had bought it and two regular angelfish, whose long delicate fins swept tranquilly through the water. The new discus was large, round, and shiny, like a silver dollar. The little gray catfish swept the bottom with his feelers, moving in and out of fresh green plants as if he were playing a game.

Near the center of the aquarium, I'd placed a large white clamshell I'd found at the ocean last summer. Next to the clamshell was Vinnie's treasure chest and a smooth black pebble Chad had given me when I refused his IOU. I propped an index card in front of the tank. The card said:

FROM YOUR SIXTH-PERIOD SCIENCE CLASS
(and Rachel P.)

Mr. Fisher was the first person into the science room after lunch. I know, because I was the second and Anne was the third. All the other kids crowded in after us, eager to witness Mr. Fisher's reaction.

He spotted the tank immediately, crossed to it, and bent to look inside. Then he picked up the index card and read it. He looked at the class, looked at the card, and then back at the class.

"I . . ." he said, his voice low and husky. "I . . ."
He cleared his throat. "Thank you."

On the far side of the room a bird twittered.
Chad snorted softly. There was a few second's silence. Then, quietly, almost apologetically, a donkey
brayed.

For the first time in Mr. Fisher's room the animal
noises were friendly.

17

I'd thought when I returned the grade book that perhaps everything else would turn out right, but life was neither fair nor simple. Despite several lower quiz scores, Jill received her A in science, and I got a C. Jill continued to act as if nothing had happened between us, but I couldn't go back to thinking of her as my friend . . . or to hating Mr. Fisher.

I wish I could say that Mr. Fisher became a good teacher and signed his contract. He did become a better teacher, at least while Mr. Marcu was visiting our class. As for signing his contract—I didn't find out about that until the very last day of the school year.

That was the day we had our awards assembly for spring sports, band, orchestra, attendance, and scholarship. There were so many awards that the assembly used up all of sixth period and part of seventh. When Mr. Marcu announced the last presentation of the afternoon, it was a bare twenty minutes before dismissal.

"This last honor is a very special one," he said, "because the student who won it has a very special record. Not only does she have a perfect A average for this year, but for every year she's been in school. We have been privileged to have her here, and wish her the best of luck for the remainder of her educational career. Students and teachers, I'm proud to present this award to Jill Ebert."

A lot of the audience applauded, but on the other side of the auditorium several kids hissed, and somebody else booed.

Two rows in front of me Vinnie yelled, "Barf!"

It was too late for detentions. Nevertheless, Mrs. Aston left her seat across the aisle to drag Vinnie from the assembly.

"Retch!" yelled Vinnie. "Aargh! Yuck!"

From somewhere behind me came a tentative, "Bawk." I glanced at Rachel, who sat beside me. Although she'd neither hissed nor applauded, she didn't look the least upset that some students were protesting Jill's award.

When the hall door had slammed shut behind Vinnie and Mrs. Aston, the principal repeated, "Jill Ebert!"

Jill walked up on the stage and crossed to the lectern, where the principal held out a hand toward her. Then he applauded, indicating that the audience should clap some more, but hardly anybody did.

Jill smiled as she shook his hand. She took the document he held out and the long white envelope containing a check from the Parent-Teacher Organization. She turned toward us and said, "I'd like to thank my teachers, who made this award possible for me."

I wondered if Jill thought at all about the fact she'd probably deserved a B one marking period in science, if she still despised Mr. Fisher, and if she missed our being best friends. Watching her accept the award, some kids might have felt jealous. But there was no envy and no admiration in me. Jill could gather A's until she graduated from high school, but that wouldn't change the fact she was a fake and a cheat.

"You may proceed to last period," Mr. Marcu told us.

Rachel and I left assembly together and headed for Mr. Gembar's room. "Mom promised I could give a party for Mary Beth when she comes to visit next week," I told her as we approached the shop.

"Want to come over this evening and help plan it?"

"Sure."

"We can have a big party at my house, or invite ten other kids for swimming and a cookout at West Lake."

"Either one sounds great," said Rachel. "I wonder if Mary Beth has changed much."

I shrugged. "I know I have."

"You even look different," said Rachel.

"How?"

"I don't know." She hesitated, then added, "Older. Prettier. You're a little quieter too, but that's all right."

Quieter. Maybe at long last I'd conquered my big mouth. Maybe not, I decided later, after dismissal, when I went to the science room. I'd only planned to tell Mr. Fisher good-bye, but that wasn't exactly all that happened.

Much to my surprise there were several other kids already talking to Mr. Fisher. I waited near the door until they'd finished, then approached him as they left the room.

"Hello, Melanie," he greeted me.

"Hi," I said. "I just came to say good-bye."

"I'm glad you did. I'll miss you next year."

"Are you going somewhere?" I blurted.

He smiled. "You are. You're going to high school."

"Then you signed your contract?"

He cocked his head and looked at me. "No, Melanie. I didn't."

"Oh." My sudden depression echoed in my voice.

"But that's not all bad." He smiled more broadly. "I've been accepted into a doctoral program at Penn State."

"You're going to be a doctor?"

"Not a medical doctor. I'm going for an advanced degree in marine biology. I haven't decided on exactly what area." He pushed back his curl. "Who knows? I might end up in teaching yet."

Somehow I doubted it—after what had happened this year. I didn't tell Mr. Fisher that, though; I just told him good-bye and good luck.

I'd missed the bus, but I didn't mind walking home. It gave me a chance to think over the past few months, to try to sort out what they had meant.

I already knew what I thought of Jill, so I concentrated on Mr. Fisher. He wasn't a very good teacher, but since he seemed happy about more years in college, maybe the school year hadn't turned out too badly for him.

As for me, Melanie . . . I sighed. I'd found out some things about myself. A few of them I didn't like very much, such as the way I'd gone along with the other kids although what they were doing was wrong—and the fact I'd been best friends with Jill even when I knew she was sneaky and couldn't be trusted.

But I'd discovered other things about me too, good things. Basically I am an honest person who tried to be fair even when I didn't want to be, when it meant giving up a friendship with someone I'd had good times with or being nice to Vinnie the repulsive. In the end I'd done my best with Mr. Fisher too, even though he hadn't signed his contract.

I'd done my best, I decided, to make up for what happened in Mr. Fisher's room—a super effort for big-mouthed, maybe not-so-ordinary Lanie.

NANCY J. HOPPER

is the author of numerous acclaimed novels for young people, many of which are set in the classroom. They include *I Was a Fifth-Grade Zebra* (Dial), *The Queen of Put-Down, The Truth or Dare Trap,* and *The Seven 1/2 Sins of Stacey Kendall.*

What Happened in Mr. Fisher's Room evolved over a period of time from Nancy Hopper's experiences as a student, a teacher, and—for the past eight years—a volunteer in the public schools. She observes, "Most of those years in school, particularly the middle ones, are involved in dealing with issues such as shifting loyalties, the consequences and meaning of friendship, and the questions of 'Who am I? What is important to me?' The middle-grader's answers to these questions very often define the person he is, and the person he will become."

Mrs. Hopper lives in Malvern, Ohio, with her husband. They have two children.